**"Don't pass out, but there's Ron Lawson,"
Ellen said out of the corner of her
mouth.**

"Where?" I practically gasped.

"Over by the big oak tree," Ellen whispered. "He's with a bunch of his friends."

I scanned the front lawn, trying not to look obvious. It's hard to do that when you really like someone, because you always end up staring at them. I guess you can figure out that I had a big crush on Ron Lawson. He's in the ninth grade, too.

Ron and I had never really had a conversation, but that was because every time I saw him I turned into a mouse. This year I was determined to be less shy. And once he saw me perform in the fall play, he was going to be convinced that we belonged together!

WHAT'S SO FUNNY ABOUT ABOUT NINTH GRADE?

Catherine Clark

Cover by Bruce Emmett

Troll Associates

Library of Congress Cataloging-in-Publication Data

Clark, Catherine, (date)
    What's so funny about ninth grade? / by Catherine Clark.
      p.   cm.—(Midway Junior High)
    Summary: Sheila loses her self-confidence as a performer and is
afraid to audition for the spring musical after her routine in the
school talent show appears to be a failure.
    ISBN 0-8167-2396-6 (lib. bdg.)   ISBN 0-8167-2397-4 (pbk.)
    [1. Talent shows—Fiction. 2. Schools—Fiction. 3. Self-
confidence—Fiction. 4. Theater—Fiction.] I. Title.
II. Series.
PZ7.C5413Wh 1992
[Fic]—dc20   91-2494

A TROLL BOOK, published by Troll Associates

Printed in the United States of America.

10 9 8 7 6 5 4 3 2

For Debbie, who made it funny.

WHAT'S SO FUNNY ABOUT NINTH GRADE?

CHAPTER

"What are *you* going to wear?" Ellen asked me.

"I don't know," I told her. "I can't decide." We were hanging out in my bedroom, trying to figure out what kind of fashion statement we wanted to make on the first day of ninth grade. You know how it is—people make up their minds about you in about two seconds on the first day of school. You have to be ready.

I was a lot more ready than last year. For one thing, I had finally gotten rid of my braces over the summer. I'd had them for two long, agonizing years.

The other thing that helped me feel ready was

that I had spent the last two weeks at Ellen's family's summer house on the beach, so I had a pretty decent tan. I'm not one of those girls who gets a golden tan, though. I have a whole bunch of little freckles on my face, and the rest of me kind of follows along.

Oh, in case you're wondering who "me" is, my name is Sheila Jenkins. I have long, red-brown hair that's seriously thick, which is supposed to be a good thing according to *Style* magazine. But it drives me crazy sometimes and I have to pull it back in a ponytail. I'm not too tall or too short or very thin or very fat— just average. I'm an only child, and I live in a small town called Greatdale.

Ellen Berret is my best friend, and has been since the third grade. She's a really good soccer player, she's skinny, and she has short blond hair. She takes things more seriously than I do, but other than that we're a lot alike. We both love pepperoni and double cheese pizza, any flavor of frozen yogurt, and Mr. Swanson, our gym teacher. He's about twenty-five years old, and he has this really cute way of yelling at us when we mess up. I should say when *I* mess up, since Ellen is Miss Coordination. The only sport I'm good at is croquet.

So anyway, we couldn't figure out what to wear. We'd gone out and bought a whole bunch of new clothes. But when school starts it's still about ninety degrees. You can't exactly go around in big sweaters and boots, unless you want to die of heat stroke.

"I think you should wear that blue-jean mini-skirt," I told Ellen.

She frowned at me. "Are you serious? I wore that the last day of school last year."

"Oh." I flopped down onto my bed. "Well, how about jeans and that big neon-painted T-shirt you have?"

Ellen straddled my desk chair and rested her chin on the back of it. "Bor-ing."

"Not necessarily. You could spray-paint your hair to match the shirt."

Ellen started giggling. "Yeah, and you could spray-paint your face to match!"

"Oh, that reminds me—do you think we should wear make-up?"

"I'm not going to," Ellen replied. "I mean, I might wear some lip gloss, but that's it."

"The only make-up I want to wear is stage make-up," I said. Midway Junior High was finally going to have a drama club, and I couldn't wait. Ever since the end of eighth grade, when the school board had announced that they'd created a budget for it, I'd been thinking of nothing else *but* the drama club. All summer I'd been reading plays and practicing my singing. My parents had even sprung for some voice lessons.

I didn't know what the production was going to be this year, but whatever it was, I was going to be in it. Even if I had only a tiny part, it would be the beginning. I planned on becoming a famous actress someday, and everyone has to start somewhere.

"Well, I don't know what I'm going to wear tomorrow, but you know what? I don't even care," Ellen said. "The most important thing is how I do at soccer practice, and I know what I'll be wearing there—shorts, a T-shirt, and cleats."

I sat up on the bed and smacked my forehead with my hand. "That's it! That's what I'll wear!"

Ellen picked up an eraser from my desk and threw it at me. "You're crazy, you know that?"

I met Ellen at my street corner about a half hour before school started. I was wearing black capri pants and a long-sleeved red-striped shirt. Ellen had on a pink and black checked shirt and black stretch pants. We always end up sort of dressing alike no matter what we say we're going to wear.

We wanted to get to school early so we could check everyone out and see who had changed over the summer.

Naturally, the first person we saw was Mrs. Biron, the assistant principal. She's a tall, heavyset Hispanic woman with short, dark hair. It didn't seem like she had changed at all. She was standing at the top of the stairs, keeping an eye on everybody. Mrs. Biron's usually pretty nice, but if you get into trouble, she does this Dr. Jekyll/Mr. Hyde routine and gives you a week of detention.

Ellen nudged me with her elbow as we got closer to the building. "Don't pass out, but there's Ron Lawson," she said out of the corner of her mouth.

"Where?" I practically gasped.

"Over by the big oak tree," Ellen whispered. "He's with a bunch of his friends."

I scanned the front lawn, trying not to look obvious. It's hard to do that when you really like someone, because you always end up staring at them. I guess you can figure out that I had a big crush on Ron Lawson. He's in the ninth grade, too.

I couldn't wait to see if we were in the same homeroom. Since our names are so close in the alphabet, you'd think we would be, but that's not how Midway does it. They just throw everyone's schedule into the computer and let it arrange things however it wants to.

I had a crush on Ron all last year. Even though I'd only seen him around town a couple of times over the summer, my feelings for him hadn't changed. He was definitely one of the best-looking guys in school. He had short brown hair, blue eyes, and a great smile. And he was funny, and nice, too.

Ron and I had never really had a conversation, but that was because every time I saw him I turned into a mouse. This year I was determined to be less shy. And once he saw me perform in the fall play, he was going to be convinced we belonged together. That was the plan, anyway.

Ellen and I moved a little closer to Ron and his group. "It's impossible," I said. "I don't believe it."

She looked at me, puzzled. "What?"

I shook my head. "He looks even better than he did last year."

Ellen shifted her knapsack to her other shoulder, casually glancing in Ron's direction as she did. "Yeah, kind of," she said.

"What do you mean, kind of? He's gorgeous!" I whispered.

"Didn't he spend the summer teaching kids to swim or something?" Ellen asked.

I nodded. Ron had a nice, dark tan, and the fact that he was wearing a white shirt didn't hurt. "I can't believe how cute he is," I said.

"Why don't you go over and say hi? You know, get the year off to a flying start and all that," Ellen suggested.

I looked at her and raised one eyebrow. "Yeah, right."

"Maybe you'll be in some of his classes," she said. "I know—you guys can be lab partners in science!"

"I'd probably get nervous and spill acid on him," I mumbled.

Ellen laughed. "No, you wouldn't. Hey, look—there's Keesha and Ruth. Let's go say hi."

"Okay," I said. Keesha Jones and Ruth Danzig are the two people Ellen and I hang out with most often. They're best friends, just like Ellen and me. Keesha has really short, dark, kinky hair, and she's into art. She paints and knows how to make ceramics, too.

I still haven't figured out what Ruth is into— definitely not school! She's kind of an airhead. Actually, she's really good at making clothes. She always comes up with the coolest outfits to wear to school. Today she was wearing a bright orange velveteen shirt and green pants that flared out at the bottom. She had on a floppy hat over her long, dark, curly hair. There was no way we could miss her!

As we headed across the lawn toward Keesha and Ruth, I turned and took one last look at Ron. I might have been dreaming, but I swear I saw him smile at me.

Yes, it was going to be a great year.

The first thing Midway does at the beginning of every year is have a big school-wide assembly. They call it the "Welcome Back Party," but there isn't much "party" to it. They give us snacks afterward, but first we have to sit through a bunch of boring lectures.

First, Mr. Glynn, the principal, ran through a list of all his expectations for us. You know, how we should be the best we can be, and make everyone in Greatdale proud of Midway. The only funny thing about his speech was when he slipped up and called the school "Mudway."

Next Mrs. Biron talked about rules and regulations. Then some of the different teams and clubs made announcements.

Finally, Mr. Blackwell, the music teacher who was going to be the adviser to the new drama club, got up on stage. I couldn't wait to hear what he was going to say about the fall play.

"The first announcement I have to make is that due to scheduling problems, we will not start the drama club until after winter break," Mr. Blackwell said with a frown.

"What?" I murmured. This was impossible! It was more than impossible—it was terrible.

"I'm sorry, people," Mr. Blackwell continued. "It's just going to take us longer than we anticipated to get ready for a big production. There's a lot of equipment we still need to purchase, as well as preparations I need to make. However, I *can* tell you that we have chosen the first musical to be performed here at Midway." He paused. "And that musical will be . . . *Grease!*" Mr. Blackwell smiled.

"All right!" I said—probably a little louder than I should have. A couple of kids turned around and stared at me. But I couldn't help it. I was excited.

"Have you read that play?" Ellen asked me.

"No, but I know the story," I told her. "It's really cool and it takes place in the '50s."

Ruth wrinkled her nose. "The 1950s or the 1850s? Because if it's the 1850s it's going to be incredibly boring. You're going to have to wear those pioneer clothes and sing about cows and horses."

I cracked up. Ruth can be pretty ditsy sometimes. "No, it's the 1950s," I told her. "Boys greased their hair back then, so that's where the title comes from. It's a big romance, plus there's all this gang-type stuff in it."

"Do you think you'll get a part?" Keesha asked.

I shrugged. "I don't know, but—"

"The auditions for *Grease* will be held in January," Mr. Blackwell said. "In the meantime, I think the social committee has an idea to keep you entertained."

Ellen squeezed my arm. At the end of eighth grade, Ron had been elected vice-president of the social committee. Naturally, I voted for him.

Ron got up and walked to the stage, and so did Marcy Wilson, the president of the committee. Marcy was in the ninth grade, too. She was always trying to run everything. We'd never been friends, which was too bad—if we had been, I would have had a way of getting to know Ron! But it wasn't worth becoming friends with Marcy just for that. She was kind of irritating. Once when I made a joke in our social studies class last year she said something like, "Really, how juvenile."

Marcy stepped in front of the microphone. "In November, the social committee will sponsor a school-wide Talent Night," she said. "Anyone can participate, but you should know one

17

very important thing." She turned to Ron and grinned. "Go ahead—it was your idea."

"Okay, well, this will be a kind of combination Talent Night and Gong Show," Ron said.

"Boy, his voice sounds deeper, doesn't it?" Keesha murmured.

I just nodded and kept looking at Ron.

"There will be four judges—including yours truly—and each will be armed with a long stick. There will be a large, *loud* gong on stage next to us. So, if someone's talent is a little . . . lacking, we can hit the gong and put the audience out of its misery," he explained. A bunch of kids started laughing.

"Of course, we hope we won't have to do that," Marcy said with a phony smile. "So start thinking about what talent you'd like to show off! We'll keep a sign-up sheet in the student council office. You should sign up in the next week because we'll need to get organized. Thanks!"

Marcy and Ron returned to their seats. Then Mr. Glynn made some final comments and dismissed us. All around me, kids were getting up and pushing their way out of the auditorium. There was free orange juice and pastries in the cafeteria for the next fifteen minutes. I love to eat, but I couldn't move. I had too much to think about.

I couldn't pass up an opportunity like this to impress Ron. The spring musical was months and months away, and what if I didn't get a part? I didn't have to audition for Talent Night—anyone could be a part of it. But what was I going to do up there?

Ellen tugged at my arm. "Earth to Sheila, Earth to Sheila," she chanted.

I looked up at her. "Did you say something?"

"Yeah. If we don't hurry up, you're not going to be able to casually bump into Ron on the way to the cafeteria," she said with a grin. "He's going by right now."

I stood up and glanced over at the aisle. Ellen was right, I had no time to lose!

The sooner I got to know Ron, the better . . . I just had to figure out *how* to do it!

CHAPTER

When I walked into English class for last period that afternoon, I practically fell over. Not because Chip Hopkins threw a paper airplane that just missed hitting me in the nose. And not because for the first time in two years Mr. Dilbert was wearing something besides a dark gray suit (this time it was navy).

Ron was sitting over by the window, in the fourth row. I had given up on finding him in any of my classes. My mom's always saying that good things happen when you're not looking for them. I decided then and there that she was right.

I walked over and sat behind him as casually

as I could. Usually I sit in the front row, so this was a big change for me. It was weird being in the back of the room . . . but I could get used to it, I thought as I listened to Ron talk to his friends. Even the back of his neck was cute.

"Hey, Ron," Dave Hiller said. "Can't you just picture the pool right now? I'd give anything to be there instead of here."

"I wish I were floating in it this very second," Ron replied, in his new, deeper voice.

And I wish I were floating right beside you, I added to myself. Now *that* would be heaven.

"Did you listen to the new Alliance disc yet?" Dave asked him.

"Yeah, it's great." Ron shook his head. "Their drummer is unbelievable. I think I heard something about them coming to the area to do a concert."

"Are you serious?" Dave asked. "Let's start camping out now for tickets."

The bell rang and I opened up my notebook— not to do any work, but to write: *Get new Alliance tape!* When Mr. Dilbert called my name for roll call, I said, "Here!" kind of loudly, so Ron would know who I was. I don't think he noticed, though.

Right away Mr. Dilbert started talking about all the assignments he was going to give us over the course of the term. He's pretty tough— I'm lucky if I get a "B" from him.

"Now, please open your textbooks to page

twelve," he said. "I'd like someone to read the poem that appears there. Any volunteers?"

Jill Branford raised her hand. "This poem is called, 'Ode to a Wounded Infantryman,' " she announced. Then she started reading it.

I followed along for a little while, but it was a long poem, and I had a lot to think about. I wanted to sign up for Talent Night as soon as possible. I figured the faster I got involved, the faster I would have an excuse to talk to Ron. But in order to sign up, I had to know what I was going to do up there in front of him . . . and four hundred other people.

I had taken ballet lessons when I was eight, but I wasn't very good. Actually, the teacher had suggested I give up ballet and try the piano instead. I was terrible at the piano. I tried the clarinet, too, but after two months of screeching and warbling, my parents brought it back to the store. So, the finer performing arts were out.

I wasn't bad at juggling but, unless you're awesome at that, it's kind of boring to watch. What else could I do? Ellen was always telling me I would make a great singer in a rock band, but I didn't have a band. Besides, I might get nervous and end up lip-synching. The idea of belting out some solo in front of Ron made my knees shake—and I was sitting down.

"Miss Jenkins, could you please pick up from there?" I suddenly heard Mr. Dilbert ask.

I looked up, startled. "What did you say?"

"Please take over the reading," Mr. Dilbert instructed. He adjusted his tie.

I glanced down at my textbook and panicked. Where in the world was I supposed to start? "Um," I said, stalling.

"We were on the line that begins, 'We, your countrymen,' " Mr. Dilbert said in an exasperated voice.

Ron turned around in his chair and before I knew what was happening, he pointed to the right line of the poem. "Here," he said. Then he turned back again.

Okay, so maybe that didn't make me look like the brightest student in the world. My face turned about twelve different shades of pink, too. But, it was a start. Ron had actually *helped* me (not to mention the fact that he had touched my book). I wasn't surprised, though—I'd known he was a nice guy all along.

School was off to an excellent start. It was going to be my year. I could feel it.

I made it through English class without any more embarrassing incidents. I tried to smile at Ron as we walked out the door together after class, but he wasn't looking at me. So much for that!

Right after English I had a meeting for the school newspaper, the Midway *Gazette*. I had written some articles for the *Gazette* in eighth grade—mostly funny stuff about where cafeteria food comes from, and why classes are thirty-nine

24

minutes long instead of forty. About fifteen students work on the paper, and it comes out twice a month.

When I walked into the *Gazette* office, the editor-in-chief, Susan Maloney, cried, "Sheila! I'm so glad you're here!"

"Hi, Susan. What's up?" I asked. Susan is a ninth grader, and she has to be the most organized person in the entire world. She keeps track of everyone's deadlines for them. Plus, she always puts in a lot of extra hours on her own to make sure the paper comes out right. Susan is also one of the shortest people in the world—I think she's still under five feet.

"We were just talking about you," Susan said.

"You were?"

"Yeah! We have a great idea for your first article this year," said Tom Schmidt, the assistant editor. He and Susan do most of the work. Tom is really nice. He's pretty cute, too. He has longish brown hair, and he always wears T-shirts with interesting messages on them. If he got rid of his black-rimmed glasses and got contacts instead, he'd be even better looking.

"How do you feel about the dress code at Midway?" Susan asked me.

I shrugged. "I didn't know there was one."

"Well, there is, and some kids are really upset about it," Tom said. "Including me. Some of the teachers don't want us to wear T-shirts anymore. We were thinking you could write an article about what's allowed and what isn't."

"You know, make a lot of funny comments about how people dress here," Susan added.

"Does this code include teachers?" I asked. "Because Mrs. Fletcher was wearing this dress today that looked like it came straight off a table at Gino's Pizzeria." Mrs. Fletcher was my guidance counselor in seventh grade.

Tom and Susan burst out laughing. "I swear, you are the funniest person at this school!" Susan giggled.

"Yeah, you should be a comedian," said Tom. "I can see it now. I'll be watching TV ten years from now, and there you'll be!"

"A comedian, huh? I guess that means I'll have to give up my dream of becoming a nuclear scientist," I said.

They cracked up all over again. You know how some people laugh at everything you say— even when it's not that funny?

Still, they *had* given me an idea. Maybe I was going to be a comedian when I got older. On second thought, maybe I was going to be one a lot sooner than that!

That night, after dinner, I called Ellen to tell her what I had decided. Since she had soccer practice all afternoon, I hadn't seen her since I'd come up with my brilliant idea. I was going to do a stand-up comedy routine for Talent Night.

"I think it's a great idea!" Ellen said enthusiastically. "You'll be terrific."

"Do you really think so? I mean, maybe you only think I'm funny because you're my best friend," I said. "Getting up on stage and telling jokes in front of a crowd is a big deal."

"Don't you remember when you used to get up and tell jokes in third grade? The whole class loved you," Ellen reminded me.

"Yeah, but that was third grade," I told her. "When you're that little, you laugh at everything."

Ellen sighed. "Come on, Sheila, you know you're funny enough to do this. Everyone loves your newspaper articles. Besides, I bet no one else will even think of doing a stand-up routine. Everyone in the audience will be sick of watching dancers and singers and stuff, so when you get up there, we'll be ready for a good laugh!"

"Does that mean you're not performing?" I asked.

"Are you kidding? The only thing I could do is dribble a soccer ball between cones," said Ellen.

"Yeah, but you'd do it better than anyone else." I grinned, imagining Ellen running around the stage, her cleats clicking on the wood floor.

"I'll leave the spotlight to you," Ellen said. "I can't wait! Do you know what you're going to say yet?"

"Of course not. I just decided about two hours ago that I'm going to do this. It's going to take me a while to come up with some good stuff."

"Well, you have over a month, right? No problem."

It's nice to have friends who have more confidence in you than you do. "Yeah, I guess it's enough time. You're going to help me, aren't you?" I asked Ellen.

"I'll laugh at all your jokes—just like always," she promised.

If only the rest of Midway Junior High liked my sense of humor as much as Ellen did, I'd have it made in the shade.

I signed up for Talent Night first thing the next day. Seeing the judges' names at the top of the sign-up sheet reminded me all over again how important it was that I *not* mess up. Ron was pretty funny himself. I knew that a bunch of boring knock-knock jokes, like the ones I used to tell when I was younger, weren't going to bowl him over. I needed to be good, really good. Not just for him, but for my future as a performer! After all, this was going to be my debut.

I spent the next month watching every funny movie, TV sitcom, and comedy routine I could get my hands on. My parents made sure I did my homework every night before I started working on my routine. They said if I was going to be a comedian I had to know about world events, which I guess is true, so I did all my social studies reading. I don't know what algebra has to do with comedy—there's nothing funny about it, if you ask me—but I did that, too.

I also got some practice by writing my column on the dress code. On the day the paper came out, Mr. Dilbert started English class by asking me where he could buy the fish tie I had suggested he wear to brighten up his wardrobe. The whole class started laughing and Ron turned around to tell me it was a great column! I was so happy I could have died.

It took me a long time to write my five-minute routine. I had a lot of trouble trying to keep myself to five minutes, but that's all I was going to get on Talent Night. I didn't want them to gong me for going over the time limit!

A week before the big performance, I asked Ellen to come over and listen to my routine.

"Don't I get some popcorn or something?" she asked, sitting down on the couch in the living room.

I shook my head. "This isn't the movies, and it's *definitely* not the circus. We can eat afterward. Right now I want you to focus on me."

Ellen leaned back on the couch and folded her arms behind her head. "Okay, show me what you've got."

I cleared my throat. I didn't know why I was so nervous. I'd always been able to make Ellen laugh. But this was different—I hadn't *planned* those jokes. I'd rehearsed my routine a few times for my parents, but that didn't count. They thought everything I did was wonderful.

"Well?" Ellen prompted. "The audience is waiting."

"Okay, okay." I glanced at my crib sheet and put on a big smile.

"Hi. It's a thrill to be here tonight—the only other time I stayed this late was in detention! Not that I deserved it. I mean, is it my fault Mr. Glynn fell over when I ran into him?"

Ellen nodded and gave me the thumbs-up sign. I've never really run into Mr. Glynn, but we comedians have to make things interesting.

"The other reason I'm glad to be here tonight is that I ate the macaroni and cheese for lunch today. I wasn't sure I was going to live through the afternoon! I think someone's been sending the stuff for the science lab to the cafeteria. Seriously, when you can divide your lunch into the table of chemical elements, you have to wonder! Did anyone see the frog legs on the menu last week?"

Ellen snickered and clapped her hands together in approval.

"All I know is, I was doing a dissection, and one day the frog was there—and the next day it wasn't!"

To tell you the truth, that hadn't really happened, either. But if the audience and the judges—one judge in particular—liked it as much as Ellen did, who cared?

"Well, what do you think?" I asked Ellen when I was finished with my routine.

"That was great!" she said in between laughs. "Not only are you going to win, you're going to be discovered by some talent scout. You'll probably spend the rest of ninth grade in Hollywood!"

I frowned at her. "Are you making fun of me?"

"No, I'm serious." Ellen stopped giggling and cleared her throat. "I think your routine is perfect. Don't change a thing."

"Do you think Ron will like it?"

"Unless he's a total dweeb, yes!" Ellen replied.

I put my hands on my hips and pretended to look shocked. "How dare you call my future boyfriend a dweeb!"

Then we both cracked up.

CHAPTER

I thought November third would never come. It seemed like months and months had passed since the day I first found out about Talent Night. I had rehearsed my act so many times, I was sick of it.

Finally, two days before Talent Night, there was a big meeting to organize all of the performers. I was psyched because I knew Ron would be there. Not that I didn't see him every day in English class, but beyond the occasional "hi," we didn't talk to each other. He had his friends, and I had mine.

When I walked into the auditorium, I was shocked. It was full of people! It seemed as if every kid at Midway was going to be performing. I had no idea so many people would want to participate. Ron wouldn't even notice me. I had to do something about that.

Taking a deep breath, I walked over to where he and Marcy were standing, near the stage. "Hi," I said, smiling. "I have a question."

Marcy looked up from the clipboard she was studying. "We'll announce the order of events in a few minutes," she said firmly. Then she went back to her clipboard. For some reason, that girl just did *not* like me.

I turned to Ron. I didn't know what I was going to say, but I had to say something. "So, how's everything going?" I asked him. "Do you think it's going to be a good show?"

He nodded. "Definitely."

I nodded, too. "I think this is a great idea. A lot of people are going to come."

"I hope so. The more people we get, the more money we make. I mean, not that *I* make any money." He smiled. "It goes into the general student activities fund."

"I didn't know you were charging people," I said.

"A dollar at the door. I think that's fair, don't you?" He had a worried look on his face.

"Oh, of course," I said. "I think that's a great idea." The minute I said that, I realized I sounded like a broken record. I couldn't help it. I turned into a babbling idiot whenever Ron was around.

"Besides, people should have to pay to watch talented people like you," Ron said. "Right?"

I couldn't believe my ears. Ron was calling me talented? He didn't even know what my act was going to be. I glanced up at him nervously, and he was still smiling at me. He had never been so nice to me before! Actually, we'd never had a conversation that was this long, either. Maybe he was this nice all the time. I wouldn't be surprised.

"Yeah, well, we try," I joked, smiling at him. I was just going to tell him about my comedy act when Mr. Blackwell ran over to us.

"Ron, we can't find one of the amplifiers. Have you seen it?" he asked.

"Yeah, it's probably backstage somewhere. I'll find it." Ron turned to me. "See you later," he said. Then he hurried off with Mr. Blackwell.

I felt like I was floating as I walked over and sat down with my classmates. Everything was going just as I had hoped. Now Ron knew who I was, and all I had to do was follow through with a terrific performance on Talent Night. No problem!

"Hi, Jessica. What are you doing for the show?" I asked Jessica McAllister, a girl from my homeroom. Jessica transferred to Midway last year and all the boys practically went crazy trying to go out with her. She has wavy auburn hair, big green eyes, and she looks like she's sixteen instead of fourteen.

"Elise and Gabrielle and I are doing a dance routine," Jessica said, pointing to her friends.

"What kind of dance routine?" I asked. "Ballet? Tap?"

"No way! We're doing a *modern* routine, you know, like a music video," she said. "I probably shouldn't tell you this, but we're doing it to San Tropez's new song," she added in a whisper.

"Wow," I said, nodding. I was impressed—and a little worried, too. Not only was Jessica gorgeous, but she was a good dancer, too. How could I compete against someone like that?

Maybe trying to be a comedian was a big mistake, I thought. For a second, I considered asking them if they needed a fourth person in their act. Then I looked up at the stage and pictured myself trying to dance to San Tropez. I'd probably fall down and ruin the whole thing.

Anyway, it was too late to change my act. I'd practiced too much and put too much into it to give up.

"Attention, everybody!" Marcy's voice boomed out of the speakers. "Let's try to keep this brief. I'm going to run through the order of performers. You don't need to memorize this—we'll post lists backstage the night of the show."

Marcy started rattling off names. She sounded like a drill sergeant. She didn't say what each person was doing, so I couldn't figure out if there were any other comedians. I didn't care if there were, so long as they didn't come before me.

My name was the twelfth one Marcy called. That was practically right in the middle. In total, there were twenty-two acts. A lot of them were groups, which is why there were so many people in the auditorium. Twelve wasn't my lucky number, but it was better than thirteen!

If I was any better at math, I guess I would have been able to figure out what my chances of winning were. I thought probably they were one in twenty-two, but that didn't account for variables like stage fright (not mine, of course) and out-of-tune pianos. I was glad the only thing *I* had to worry about was me!

I was also glad that I didn't have to worry so much about Ron anymore. I kind of got the feeling he liked me. I know I didn't have much to go on, but hey, you have to think positively. And I was positive that Talent Night was going to be a total success!

No matter how long I live, even if I'm one of those people who celebrates her one-hundredth birthday on TV, I'll always remember Friday, November third.

My parents made a special dinner for me, but I was too nervous to eat much. I had picked out my outfit a few weeks earlier, so getting dressed was no big deal. I was wearing a red shirt with a colorful brocade vest over it, and tan jeans. I wasn't a professional comedian yet, but I knew one thing: the audience wasn't sup- posed to laugh at what you were wearing!

Ellen came over to help me get ready. "Just think, you're going to look back at tonight as the beginning of your career," she said as she watched me brush my hair in front of my bedroom mirror.

"And *you* were there," I said. "Right?"

"Well, I guess it wouldn't hurt if you happened to mention that in your book," she said.

"What book?" I asked.

"The one you're going to write when you're famous. Everyone does it."

I turned to look at her. "It's only one little Talent Night. I'm not exactly ready for stardom yet. Besides, no one says I'm going to win."

"*I* say you're going to win," Ellen said. "And, as you know, I am always right."

I looked at her in the mirror and raised my eyebrows. "Except for the few hundred times you've been wrong."

"Look, do you want to win or not?" she asked.

"Of course I do," I said.

"Then you have to think positively," she said. "Coach Green says that half of winning is thinking like a winner. So, say you're going to win." She took the brush out of my hand and tapped me on the shoulder with it. "Go ahead, say it."

"I'm going to win," I mumbled.

"Say it like you mean it!"

"Ellen, this isn't a soccer huddle," I reminded

her. "I'm not going to chant B-E A-G-G-R-E-S-S-I-V-E."

"Well, you should," she said matter-of-factly. "It works for me."

"How about this? I will B-E F-U-N-N-Y!" I cried, throwing my fist into the air. Unfortunately, Ellen was leaning forward at that moment, and my fist caught her squarely on the chin.

"Well, other than the fact that you almost knocked me out, I'd say it's an excellent slogan," she said, rubbing her chin. "I think you need to work on your timing, though."

"Ellen! You never say that to a struggling comedian," I told her. "My timing is *perfect*. I was just delivering the punch line—get it?" I chuckled.

Ellen groaned. "Do you have any aspirin?"

I don't know if you believe in omens and stuff like that. I don't really, but it *did* seem like the evening was off to a bad start.

Before the show started I peeked through the curtains and saw Ellen, Ruth, and Keesha sitting together in the third row. Ellen didn't look like she was in pain, and I was glad. My parents were sitting a few rows behind them. The auditorium was packed.

"Ready?" a voice behind me asked. I practically fell over from shock. It was Ron!

"Yeah, I guess so," I said, turning around.

Then I remembered Ellen's advice: think positively! "I mean, yes, I'm definitely ready," I told Ron with a smile. I wondered if he'd even noticed that I no longer had braces.

"Good, because this thing is definitely about to start," he said, glancing out at the crowd. He looked good, as usual—he was wearing a black tuxedo jacket over a white T-shirt, jeans, and high-tops. He had a red carnation sticking out of his jacket pocket—all the judges were supposed to wear them.

"The auditorium's practically full," I said. "This should bring in a lot of money."

"Yeah, I'm psyched," said Ron. "Maybe we'll be able to get a good band for one of our parties."

"How about Alliance?" I said, laughing. "You never know, they might want to add Midway Junior High to their tour. Right in between New York and London."

Ron burst out laughing. "That'll be the day."

"Well, we could *try*," I said with a shrug.

"We'll probably end up with someone's older brother and his band," Ron said, shaking his head. "Maybe we should spend the money on food instead."

"Good plan," I said.

Out of the corner of my eye, I saw Marcy approaching with the other two judges, Mr. Blackwell and Mrs. Biron.

"All set, Ron?" Marcy asked.

"Sure thing," said Ron.

40

"Would you mind moving over to the wings?" Mr. Blackwell asked me. "It's time to get this show on the road."

I nodded and started to walk away.

"Hey, good luck!" Ron called out just as the curtains opened.

I whirled around to see if he was talking to me, but it was too late—the crowd was cheering and the judges were already out on stage. I took my place in the wings with the rest of the acts.

Everyone was more dressed up than I was. Jessica, Elise, and Gabrielle were wearing matching ripped-up, faded blue jeans and bright orange, pink, and green T-shirts. That might not sound very dressed up, but it was— they looked great.

One guy was wearing a black tux and he had a big top hat and a wand in his hand, so I figured he was doing a magic act. A couple of girls had on long skirts and fancy blouses. A group of guys was doing a dance, too, according to Jessica. They wore matching bomber jackets and black jeans. Suddenly it seemed like everyone was more prepared—and more talented— than I was!

"Welcome to Talent Night!" Marcy cried, and the audience applauded. "Here's how this works. Each judge will score every act on a scale of one to ten, with categories for poise, originality, stage presence, and, of course, talent! The scores will be tallied at the end of the night, and the person with the most points will win!"

"But," Ron interjected, "if we find any act unbearable to sit through, never fear—the gong is here!" He waved a baton in the air, and then struck the large, gold gong with it. The audience roared with laughter. Ron and Marcy sat down at the judges' table.

Mrs. Biron asked the audience to be polite, and said she didn't want any heckling.

Then Mr. Blackwell stepped up to the microphone and said, "May the best act win!" He and Mrs. Biron took their seats.

I looked at Jessica and rolled my eyes. She giggled.

Marcy had a microphone at her chair, since she was the head judge. She tapped it with one finger to see if it was working. Then she said, "Our first performer is . . . Jackie Smith!"

A girl I didn't know ran out onto the stage, and the pianist started playing a song from a recent Broadway musical. The girl's first few words were so soft you could barely hear them. I guess she figured that out, so she belted out the next line—completely out of tune. I sat down on one of the little metal chairs backstage and prepared myself for a long night.

A little later, I was watching a magician try to pull a rabbit out of his hat. He reached in and pulled out an egg instead—which promptly burst in his gloved hand. The audience burst out laughing, and Marcy walked over to the gong and hit it. I felt sorry for the guy—he was the first one to get gonged.

Still, better him than me, I thought. To make sure I wouldn't bomb I pushed up my sleeve and glanced at my routine. I had written key words on my wrist to remind me of all my jokes. As if I could forget them, I said to myself. I could recite that routine in my sleep.

I had to sit through two renditions of a top forty love song, a ballet solo, and a scene from *Hamlet* before it was my turn. I was getting so antsy, I got up and started pacing while I waited. I couldn't wait to hear the crowd crack up at my jokes, and to see Ron's reaction when he realized how funny I was. I was more ready for this than I had been for anything in my life.

Finally, the guy ahead of me finished reciting his "To be or not to be" monologue, and ran off the stage. If *he* didn't get the gong, I thought to myself, there was no way I would!

Jessica squeezed my arm as the audience finished applauding. I took a deep breath and fixed my sleeve so I could see my notes, just in case. I didn't think anyone would notice them. I had written very small.

"Our next act is in the ninth grade. Please welcome . . . Sheila Jenkins!"

I stepped out onto the stage. It wasn't anything like I'd pictured it. There were bright lights shining right in my face, and I couldn't see anyone in the audience. I could hear a bunch of people cheering and calling my name, but it seemed like they were a thousand miles away. The gong was right behind me, and it looked as big as our kitchen table. The judges were on my left and they were all staring at me, including Ron.

I made my way over to the microphone. Well, here goes everything, I thought, trying to smile. B-E F-U-N-N-Y!

CHAPTER 4

"Hi," I said meekly into the microphone. "It's great to, uh, be here." I glanced at my wrist to find out what I was supposed to say next. But I couldn't read what I had written! My handwriting was so small it was practically invisible. The only way to read it would be to hold my wrist up to my face, which would be totally obvious and geeklike. I had to remember my first line—and fast! Out of the corner of my eye I saw Marcy tapping her pencil on the table.

"Um, actually I'm glad we're all here," I said. No, that wasn't it, I told myself. I could hear people in the audience moving around. "Did anyone else eat the frog legs for lunch today?"

Nobody laughed. I had messed up the whole joke. Well, it was only one—I could make up for it with the next one. If only I could remember what the next joke was . . .

"Did you all hear about the new dress code?" I asked, stalling until I could remember my real routine. "We're not allowed to wear anything plaid or striped at the same time. I guess that means Mr. Glynn will have to get a whole new wardrobe!" A few giggles rippled through the crowd. Mr. Glynn's clothes are so uncoordinated, it's funny. But I guess it's not *that* funny.

Suddenly I remembered my first big joke. "You know, that reminds me," I said, looking around casually and feeling more relaxed. "I was walking down the hall yesterday and I saw two seventh graders trying to open their lockers. One of them says, 'How do you work this thing?' and the other says, 'I don't know, I only go to school here.' " I heard one person in the audience laugh—probably Ellen. I pictured a mob of seventh graders waiting to beat me up in the parking lot.

I had to keep going. I had to get at least one good joke in before my five minutes were up! It seemed as if I had been on stage for an hour, and I knew my chances of winning were fading fast.

"But seriously," I said, mustering a grin, "have you ever thought about what actually goes into the school's macaroni and cheese? I heard that the janitors were missing a ten-gallon drum of floor cleaner. Coincidence or fact? You be the judge," I said, making a face.

This time I heard a whole bunch of people laughing. Whew! "All I know is, the floors around here are looking pretty dirty, and the dishwasher was fired—they don't need him anymore, because the plates clean themselves!" I continued. Finally, I was on a roll. It felt good to know everyone was laughing at my jokes. I even thought I heard Ron chuckle once or twice.

"Actually, I shouldn't be so hard on the cafeteria," I said, shrugging. "They do the best they can. Their best just happens to be *horrible*. I've started bringing my own lunch. The only problem is, the home ec people won't let me use the microwave. I guess they think I'm going to ruin it—something about my lunch being wrapped in tin foil. Can I help it if—"

Suddenly, I was interrupted by a loud "GONGGGGGGG!" I spun around to the judges' table. There was Ron, holding the baton and grinning. I practically collapsed right there. But I was so stunned, I couldn't move. Hadn't people been laughing at my routine? Or had I just imagined that?

I wanted to die. A couple of people in the audience booed. They hated me!

I turned and ran off the stage into the wings.

"Tough break," I heard Jessica say, but I didn't stick around to discuss it. I couldn't get out of that auditorium fast enough!

"How did you get home?" Ellen asked when she called me later that night.

"I walked, of course," I said.

"I thought your parents wouldn't let you walk alone after dark," she said.

"Well, I wasn't about to wait around for them," I said glumly. "I didn't exactly feel like mingling with everyone after the show, if you know what I mean."

"Sheila, you really did a good job up there!" Ellen argued.

"Sure," I said, nodding. "That's why Ron hit the gong so hard. It practically shattered."

"He did not. Anyway, I don't know what his problem is. Everyone around me was laughing really hard at your jokes," said Ellen.

"I doubt that," I said. I let out a big sigh. "I really messed up. But why am I telling *you* that? You heard me—I forgot all the jokes I had practiced!"

"So what? The ones you came up with were fine."

"Obviously not. Look, can you do me a big favor?" I asked.

"Sure, anything," Ellen replied.

"On Monday, can you tell Mr. Glynn that I won't be coming to school anymore? I've decided to do all my studying at home from now on.

No, wait—I think I'll see if my parents want to move to another country. I've always liked the idea of France," I said, half-joking, but half-serious, too.

There was no way I could go back to Midway Junior High—at least not in this lifetime. "We're going away this weekend. Maybe we won't come back," I said wistfully. If only I could convince my parents. . .

"Cut it out, Sheila—you're not moving any-where," Ellen said, laughing. "Besides, you don't even speak French."

"I could learn," I argued.

"I'll meet you at the corner on Monday, same time as always," Ellen said. "Only don't be late like you usually are."

"Are you sure you want to be seen with me?" I asked her. "I mean, I understand if you—"

Ellen hit one of the touchtone buttons, and it beeped in my ear. "I'm saying good night now, Sheila."

"Wait a second! Aren't you even going to tell me who won?" I asked. I had to know, even if it killed me.

"It was a tie between two acts who went after you. There was a girl who sang incredibly well. She's in the eighth grade, and I think her name is Wendy. The other act was a group of guys wearing jeans and bomber jackets who danced. They were excellent!" She paused. "Sorry. You were good, too."

We said good night and I hung up the phone.

As I got into bed, I glanced at the clock. It was eleven-thirty. In only half an hour, the worst day of my life would be over. I couldn't wait.

Then again, maybe Monday would be even worse. I had to face everyone who had seen me make an idiot of myself. In my mind, there was nothing worse than someone trying to be funny who wasn't. You've seen bad TV shows and actors, so you know what I mean. I honestly didn't know how I was going to do it.

I was glad we were going out of town to visit my grandmother. At least I wouldn't run into anyone I knew.

You know how when you listen to really loud music at a concert, your ears keep ringing afterward? Well, the sound of that stupid gong kept ringing in my ears. I turned on my clock radio so I could hear something else, but there was someone singing about a broken heart, so I turned it off. I couldn't take that, not after what had happened.

I couldn't fall asleep for a long time. I kept thinking about how *glad* Ron had looked when he'd hit that gong. Maybe he was just trying to get into the spirit of the thing. I guess I had been pretty bad, but I couldn't understand why, after all the practicing I had done. Was there such a thing as being *too* ready?

Maybe I had panicked because I wanted to do so well in front of Ron. Great, just great. The one person I wanted to like my act *hated* it. He couldn't even stand to listen to the rest of my routine.

When the grandfather clock in the living room struck midnight, I rolled over and sighed. If I never heard of Talent Night again, I'd be happy.

Monday morning when I got up, I felt terrible. After I got dressed, I went into the bathroom to fix my hair. I looked as bad as I felt! I hadn't fallen asleep until around three, and I had big puffy circles under my eyes.

That gave me an idea—a very good idea. I didn't have to worry about what would happen at school that day—because I wasn't going!

I trudged downstairs to the kitchen, moving as slowly as possible and trying to look extremely pathetic.

"Mom, I don't feel good," I whined, slouching over to her. I took my mother's hand and held it up to my throat. "Feel that big lump there? I must have swollen glands."

She rubbed my throat a few times. "I don't feel anything."

"I'm telling you, it's not normal," I said, sitting down at the kitchen table next to my father. "I think I'd better stay home today. It might be something serious."

"I'll tell you what's not normal—you!" my mother said with a laugh. "Honestly, Sheila, you've been trying that same thing for years. Don't you think we've caught on by now?"

"I'm sure you're just fine," my father said, patting me on the back.

I cleared my throat loudly. "I don't know, it feels kind of funny." Just saying that word made me cringe—if there was anything in the world I was not, it was funny!

Mom filled a glass with orange juice and handed it to me. "Here, drink this. It has all the vitamin B you need."

I took a sip. "Don't you mean vitamin C?"

"No, I mean B. For bravery," she said, sitting down at the table. "I know it's not going to be easy for you to go to school today, after what happened Friday night. But you can do it."

"Do I have to?" I groaned. "Everyone's going to tease me."

"Don't worry about what other people are saying about you," my father advised. "We know you weren't pleased with your performance, but it was *fine*, Sheila. A lot of kids were cracking up!"

"Yeah, because I looked so dumb," I said.

"No, because they liked your jokes!" my mother insisted. They had been telling me the same thing all weekend, only every time they brought the subject up, I told them I didn't want to talk about it.

"If you see that judge with the bad sense of humor, just pretend he doesn't exist," my father said as he buttered a piece of toast.

"Yes, don't give him a second thought,"

added my mother. Obviously, they had no idea how much I liked Ron.

"I'll try," I said. My stomach turned over at the thought of running into Ron. I could hide from him all day, if it weren't for English class. But I had a plan to take care of that. Before homeroom I was going to ask Mrs. Biron to switch my schedule around.

"Now that that's settled, what can I get you for breakfast?" Mom asked.

"Do you have any paper bags left over from the supermarket?"

She stared at me. "Why?"

I stood up and put on my jacket. "I need to wear one over my head!"

Both Mom and Dad cracked up laughing. As I went out the front door, my father shouted, "You really should have won the other night!"

Being the funniest person in your house doesn't count for much of anything, I wanted to tell him. If my parents ever started gonging me, then I'd really be in trouble. I could just see my dad holding up a big frying pan and whacking it with a spoon.

That thought made me smile. I was still smiling when I got to the corner and saw Ellen waiting for me.

"You look like you're in a good mood," she said.

"I'm just practicing my acting," I told her. "I have to act like everything's okay, or I'll die of embarrassment today."

"Sheila, you have nothing to be embarrassed about," said Ellen. "Besides, you can knock everyone dead in your next stage appearance."

"Don't hold your breath," I warned her. "I don't know if I'll ever appear on stage again! Not for at least a million years, anyway."

"Yeah, right. You're going to be in *Grease*, remember?" Ellen asked me. "I'm looking forward to being the best friend of a celebrity. In the meantime, though, we have to get to school before the warning bell."

"Why don't you go on ahead without me? I'll catch up later," I said. I was thinking of going home and hiding in the garage for the day.

Ellen grabbed my arm and started pulling me down the sidewalk. "Come on. Don't you want to see Ron?"

I raised one eyebrow and stared at her.

"Sorry—bad question," Ellen said, looking sheepish.

"He's the last person I want to see," I said. "I'd rather run into a wild boar than see him."

"Well, there aren't any wild boars in Great-dale, so you're out of luck," Ellen said. "Just remember, if he can't see what a great person you are, it's his loss."

His loss? Hardly! It was my loss—and my humiliation, too. Kind of a package deal.

I didn't know how I was going to make it through the day. Ellen was taller than me. . . maybe I could hide behind her.

In any case, it was not going to be easy!

CHAPTER

When I walked into homeroom that morning, I kept my head down. I didn't want to look at anybody . . . or see anybody looking at me.

So far, the morning was off to a rotten start. Mrs. Biron had listened politely to my reason for wanting to change my schedule. I told her I'd do better in algebra if it was last period, because I could concentrate really well at the end of the day. She thought it over for a minute or so and then said "No." She also said she didn't want to discuss the matter further. I don't think I caught her in one of her good moods.

I slunk into my seat and opened a notebook right away, so I'd look busy. Actually, I *was* busy. I had to finish all the homework I hadn't done over the weekend because I'd been too upset to work on anything.

Jessica McAllister came in and sat next to me. "Hi, Sheila," she said. She gave me a sympathetic smile.

I hate it when people are extra nice to you because they feel sorry for you. "Hi," I said, still staring into my notebook.

"How come you didn't stick around on Friday night?" she asked.

Was she crazy? "I didn't feel like it," I said. "After, well, you know."

"After you got gonged, you mean?"

Why don't you say it a little louder? Maybe everyone in the room wasn't there, I thought angrily. "Yeah," I muttered.

"Well, you should have been there—you missed seeing our act." Jessica giggled. "I still can't believe what happened."

I looked up at her. "What?"

"Well, there was this one part of our dance when we were all supposed to go to the right— only I went left instead, and I rammed right into Elise. She fell down," Jessica whispered, "and I landed on top of her! It was *terrible*."

I shook my head. "Not as terrible as making a bunch of lame jokes."

"Are you kidding? I've never seen Mr. Blackwell move as fast as he did to hit that gong. It was humiliating."

56

"I bet it wasn't that bad," I told her. "You probably looked good before that happened."

"No, not really. We kept missing the jumps we'd practiced, and my shoe came off once, too." Jessica shook her head. "I'll never try to dance in public again."

"I thought you were auditioning for *Grease*," I said. The sign-up sheets had been posted November first, but the auditions weren't until January. I had put my name on the list, but I wasn't sure it was going to stay there.

"Oh, sure, I'll do that," Jessica said. "That's a long way away. No one will remember what a doofus I was on Talent Night."

Easy for you to say, I thought.

"You're auditioning too, aren't you?" asked Jessica.

I looked at her and shrugged as Mr. Blake walked into the room. "Maybe, maybe not," I said. The way things were going, the odds were better than one in twenty-two that I would *not* have the lead—or any part at all—in the spring musical.

The rest of the morning passed fairly uneventfully, so I was feeling pretty good by the time lunch rolled around. I had brought my lunch that day, so I was the first one to get to our usual table in the cafeteria.

Ellen had biology class right before lunch. I figured she was probably going over her homework with the teacher, and got out my sandwich. Ruth and Keesha came over a few minutes later, after getting their lunches.

"Hi!" Ruth said. "What's up?"

"Nothing much," I told her. I was starving, so I took a big bite of my peanut butter sandwich. Then I realized what was missing from my lunch. I needed something to drink. "I'm going to get some milk. Do you guys want anything?" I asked.

"Oh, I meant to get some Jell-O," said Keesha. "It's the only thing they *can't* mess up. Can you get me some?"

"Sure, what flavor? Lame Lime, 'Orrible Orange, or Choke Cherry?" I asked. We made up names for the Jell-O in seventh grade, and the flavors had never changed.

"Lame Lime," Keesha replied. "And get one with a lot of whipped cream."

I walked up to the line and grabbed a carton of milk and the dish of Jell-O. I was on my way back to our table when I heard some guy say, "There goes the cafeteria critic."

I ignored him and kept walking. There was one crowded section where all the guys on the soccer team sat, and I had to squeeze in between two tables. I was trying to get past when Pete Phelan said, "Hey, look, it's the girl who forgot to bring her jokes the other night!"

"I thought you had to have *talent* to get up there," Chip Hopkins added.

Pete started laughing. "Obviously not!"

I was blushing so much, I could even feel my ears getting hot. I should have known I wasn't going to make it through the day without someone making fun of me.

"You know, Sheila, maybe you should have signed up to do another act—the one where you make your ears turn red! You're really good at that!" John Corcoran yelled, and everyone at the table started laughing.

I felt like throwing the bowl of Jell-O at them, but I just shoved in a chair so I could get by. I made it back to the table without anyone else saying anything.

"I'm going to eat outside," I said, putting the Jell-O on Keesha's tray.

"Sheila, it's thirty degrees out," Ruth said. "You can't eat out there. Your milk will turn into ice cream."

"Good, I like ice cream," I told her. I grabbed my stuff and went out into the hall, then outside onto the front steps. It was pretty cold on the stone steps, so I sat on my algebra book. I knew I should go back inside and get my coat, but I didn't want to run into anyone in the hall. Besides, I thought that if I stayed outside, maybe I'd get pneumonia or something, and then I wouldn't be able to come to school for weeks—maybe even months!

I couldn't eat my sandwich. Not only because peanut butter gets even harder to eat when it's frozen, but also because I felt so miserable. It wasn't just those jerks on the soccer team, it was everyone. Either they were laughing at me, or they were feeling sorry for me. No one had forgotten what had happened, and no one was *going* to.

There was no way I could walk into English class and sit behind Ron like I usually did. He didn't think I was funny. He thought *I* was a joke. I knew his opinion shouldn't matter so much to me, but it did, and I couldn't change that.

Now I would never get to know him better. He would avoid me like the plague. Tears welled up in my eyes as I thought about all the hopes I'd had for ninth grade. Now it was all ruined. Ninth grade was a total flop, and I still had to live through the rest of the year!

"What in the world are you doing out here?"

I looked up, and when I did a tear trickled down my cheek.

"Hey, what's wrong?" Ellen sat down beside me. She pulled a tissue out of her knapsack and handed it to me. "You don't want to have icicles on your face, do you?"

I smiled. Ellen always knew what to say. I wiped my eyes and said, "Thanks."

"So, did you decide to work on your winter tan? Or did something happen that I don't know about?"

I sniffled. "Some guys on the soccer team made fun of me."

"So?" Ellen scoffed. "What else is new?"

She had a point. The guys in our class are always teasing us for some reason or other. My mom says it's a phase boys go through, but I didn't see it ending any time soon. "Yeah, but—"

"But nothing." Ellen rubbed her arms. "Let's go back inside."

"Ellen, I can't," I told her.

"Yes, you can," she said, standing up. "If anyone gives you a hard time, I'll try out my new cleats on them."

"Promise?"

"Promise," she said. "Now get up before I have to take you to the nurse for frostbite."

I stood up and tossed my half-frozen sandwich into the trash can just as the bell rang. "So much for lunch," I said with a shrug.

"Only three more classes to go," Ellen said, pulling open the big front door.

I wasn't even thinking about my other two classes. The only one that mattered to me was English.

At five minutes to two I stood outside the classroom. I put off going inside as long as possible, but when I spotted Mr. Dilbert walking down the hall, I knew it was time to bite the bullet. If I was late, it would only draw more attention to me.

I took a deep breath and opened the door. Ron was talking to his friends, as usual. I didn't even want to look at him long enough to check out what he was wearing. I slipped into a seat near the door, and Mr. Dilbert walked into the room a few minutes after me.

Mr. Dilbert took attendance first. When he called my name, he looked at the row where I normally sat. "Sheila must be out sick today," he muttered, jotting something down in his book.

I wish, I thought. "No, I'm, uh, here," I said.

Mr. Dilbert turned to look at me. "What are you doing all the way over there?" he said with a smile.

I *was* trying to hide, I wanted to say. I just shrugged my shoulders. I knew Ron must be looking at me—or else trying not to, because he was so embarrassed for me. I heard someone in the back of the room laugh, and I knew it was me that was so amusing.

After Mr. Dilbert finished roll call, he said, "I thought we'd bring the play we're reading to life today."

I closed my eyes. Oh, no, I said to myself. Not today. Please!

"It helps us understand drama when we see it performed, since that's how it is intended to be perceived," Mr. Dilbert explained.

Can't we just see the movie, I wanted to ask.

"So, I need four people up here, to start off. Let's see . . . why don't I start with that side of the room?" He pointed in my direction. "Mark, Will, Iris, and Sheila, come on up, and bring your books."

Naturally, I had picked the wrong day to

switch seats. I stood up with the others, still avoiding Ron's eyes.

We had been assigned to read the first two acts of a modern play about a famous court case in the South. I had only read the first few pages, though.

I got the part of this old woman who testified at the trial. Mr. Dilbert had me sit at his desk and pretend it was the witness stand. A week ago, I would have loved to get up there and act my heart out. But now . . .

I didn't have to say anything for a while, and my attention drifted a little. I started thinking about how Talent Night *should* have gone. I pictured Ron holding his stomach, he was laughing so hard. Marcy was howling into the microphone, and people were rolling in the aisles. Afterward, I signed a few autographs and—

"Please state your name and occupation." Mark was standing right in front of me, giving me a very serious look.

"Uh, Sheila J—I mean, Natalie Collins, sir," I said quickly, glancing at my book. I heard some giggling in the room. "I am a dressmaker," I said, trying to affect a Southern accent.

"No, you're not," Mark said. "Look!" He pointed to the text. "You're a phone operator. Iris is a dressmaker."

"Lying in court is a federal offense!" Dave, one of Ron's friends, called out. "Put the old lady away!" The rest of the class cracked up.

I felt my face go from pink to hot pink to ruby red.

"Okay, people, let's get back to the play," Mr. Dilbert instructed us. "Sheila, continue. Nice job with the accent—it sounds very authentic."

For a second I thought about moving down South. According to Mr. Dilbert, I would fit right in—which was more than I could say for Midway.

The rest of the class was torture. I couldn't stand performing in front of Ron again. I kept expecting him to stand up and smack his shoe on the desk to get me to stop.

When the bell rang, I stuffed my book in my knapsack and headed for the door. I couldn't get out of there fast enough. I was halfway down the hall when I heard someone calling my name.

"Sheila! Hey, Sheila!"

I looked over my shoulder and saw Ron hurrying toward me. His friends were right behind him. "Wait up, I want to talk to you!" Ron called.

Did he think I was stupid or something? There was no way I was going to wait for him to catch up with me so he and his friends could make fun of me again! I ducked into the girls' bathroom and waited for about five minutes, until I was sure they were gone.

On my way out of school after English class, I stopped by the student council office and crossed my name off the audition list for *Grease*.

It was the smartest thing I had done in weeks.

CHAPTER

"**Y**ou did *what*?" Ellen cried when I talked to her that night on the telephone.

"I crossed my name off the audition list," I said calmly.

"Sheila, that's crazy! You haven't stopped talking about the spring musical. You said, and I quote, 'This play is going to be the best thing that's ever happened to me.' "

"Well, that was before the *worst* thing that ever happened to me," I told her. "I'm just not ready to go on stage. No, scratch that. I've decided to give up acting, for good."

"How can you give it up when you've never even tried it?" asked Ellen.

"Trust me—I'm never going to be good at it," I said. "And I'm not going to humiliate myself again."

Ellen sighed. "How many times do I have to tell you, you didn't humiliate yourself?"

"Look, Ellen, I heard those people booing me, okay? I don't want to talk about this anymore. My decision is final," I said.

"Okay, but I think you're making a big mistake," said Ellen.

"Whatever," I said.

"Well, are you coming to my game this Saturday?" she asked. "It's in Marshfield, and my mom and dad want to know if you need to catch a ride with them."

Usually I go to all of Ellen's games. This year she was doing really well—she'd already scored twelve goals, which was close to the school record. But after that day, I didn't want to leave the house unless I absolutely had to. "Is the boys' team playing there, too?" I asked.

"Sure, as usual," she replied.

"I don't know, I might have to help my parents clean out the garage," I lied.

"Can't you get out of it?"

"I don't think so. They've been threatening to throw out anything that's mine if I don't help."

"Oh. Well, I guess I'll see you tomorrow. I still think you should reconsider auditioning for *Grease*. Bye!"

I hung up the phone and opened the refrigerator. All this arguing had made me hungry. I was scooping some chocolate ice cream into a bowl when my mother walked in.

"Hi there," she said, taking a bowl out of the cupboard. "Would you mind filling this, too? I could use a break." My mother is a freelance journalist and she works at home, which is great because she can choose her own hours. She has an office right off the kitchen.

"Sheila, I don't want you to think I was eavesdropping, but I thought I heard you say something about the auditions. Are they coming up soon?" she asked me.

I nodded and felt the ice cream slide down my throat. "They're in January."

"Are you looking forward to them?"

I shrugged. "It doesn't really matter to me."

My mother looked like she was about to choke. "What—what did you say?"

"The auditions don't matter to me. I hope they cast good people and everything, sure, but—"

"Sheila, aren't *you* auditioning?"

"Nope," I said, eating another spoonful of ice cream. I felt more relaxed than I had in weeks, sitting there in the warm kitchen with my feet up on a chair.

"Does this have anything to do with Friday night?" She started twirling her spoon around in the bowl.

"Yes and no. I just don't think I'm meant for the stage. I'll find something else to do. Don't worry—it won't be the clarinet."

"But you practiced so hard all summer! You're *good*," my mother said. "Don't give up because of one bad experience."

"I'm not giving up!" I said. I hate it when people accuse me of being a quitter. "I'm just . . . waiting. When the right play comes along, maybe I'll audition."

"I thought you loved *Grease*." My mother was staring at me with a confused look on her face, the one she got whenever I made decisions without consulting her and Dad first.

"It's okay," I said. The truth was, I did love that play. I just didn't love the idea of me being in it . . . and ruining it. "Well, I have to finish my homework, Mom." I stood up and put my bowl in the dishwasher. My mother just kept sitting there at the table, looking sad.

I couldn't understand why everyone was so upset about my decision to drop out of the auditions. I thought they would be *glad* they wouldn't have to sit through another agonizing performance of mine. Besides, I had certainly had enough humiliation for one lifetime.

The next few weeks crept along. I couldn't wait for Thanksgiving, because we had four days off. I don't know how I made it through English class every day. I pretended I had blinders on, so I couldn't even *see* Ron and be reminded of how cute he was and what a dope I had been.

After that first day, no one made fun of me—

not that I heard, anyway. But I was sure kids were still laughing at me. When I got called on in class I wanted to slip under my desk and vanish into thin air. My friends said I was being silly when I told them I couldn't do stuff like go to football games and rallies. But they didn't know what torture it was for me.

My goal was to become invisible. I started wearing really boring clothes so I wouldn't stand out in a crowd. I also stopped writing articles for the newspaper. I figured people would forget about me if they didn't see my name in print.

I used to make a lot of comments in my classes, and I guess most of them were on the humorous side. I stopped doing that, too. I was probably the only one who appreciated them. I didn't want everyone looking at me and thinking, "She is *so* not funny."

A few days before Thanksgiving break I ran into Susan Maloney, the *Gazette* editor. Actually, she came to my homeroom before school started.

"Sheila, hi! Where have you been?" she asked. "I never see you around anymore." She sat down at the desk next to mine.

"I've been around," I said.

"Well, you haven't been to any of our meetings, so I was worried about you. You still want to write for the paper, don't you?"

"I don't know. I've been thinking about it and—"

"You *can't* say no," Susan said, shaking her head. "You're the best writer we have! The paper is totally boring without you. Don't tell me you haven't noticed that."

I smiled. "Well . . . I didn't want to say anything, but it has seemed kind of weak."

"So why don't you want to write anymore?" Susan asked.

"It's not that I don't want to write. It's just . . . well, I'm kind of trying to stay out of the spotlight." I wrinkled my nose. "You know."

Susan shook her head again. "No, I don't know."

"Remember? Talent Night," I whispered.

"What?" Susan tapped her chin as she thought about it. "Are you talking about that thing that was a couple of months ago?"

"It was twenty-three days ago, actually," I told her.

"Yeah, and? What about it? Oh, I guess our article about it *was* kind of boring."

"It's not that. Susan, don't you remember? I was the act without any talent." I gave her a knowing look. "I'm not so sure you should have me on the newspaper staff anymore."

Susan laughed. "Don't be ridiculous! We need you, desperately. You write the funniest, most interesting articles, and you know it. So, what are you going to write about for next week?"

I hesitated. I did miss writing for the paper. But I didn't want my name in print. Then I got a brilliant idea. "Susan, I'll write whatever you want me to, under one condition."

"Name it," she said.

"It has to be published under a phony name, so no one knows it's me."

"You mean a pseudonym?"

I nodded. "Right."

"But Sheila, people look for your articles in the paper. What's the point of not using your name? If you do that, no one will read your article. And if they like it, they won't even know it's yours."

"Do you want me to write the article or not?" I countered.

Susan stood up as the warning bell rang. "Okay, have it your way. But I hope this isn't going to last long."

"What should I do the article on?" I asked her.

"Whatever you want," she said, heading toward the door. Then she turned around. "Why don't you write about people who change their names?"

"Ha ha," I said, rolling my eyes.

She laughed. "See you later!"

I worked on my article the Sunday night before Thanksgiving break was over. It wasn't due until the end of the week, but I thought I'd get an early start. In case anyone found out who Daisy Pritchard was, I wanted to make sure the thing was at least readable.

I didn't know what to write about. Not much had happened at school recently. Christmas was coming, but that was old news. I thought about doing a critique of Thanksgiving dinner—why *do* we eat so much food, anyway?—but that seemed boring. Then I thought maybe I'd discuss the fact that no good movies had come out since the summer.

I kept thinking about the people who might be in *Grease*. I wondered if Ron was going to watch the auditions. He might want to help Mr. Blackwell decide who had talent and who didn't, since he was such an expert.

I jotted an idea for an article in my notebook. *Gong-Happy Judges: What's Their Problem?*

Just then the phone rang, and I ran out into the hall to get it. "Hello?" I said.

"Hi." It was Ellen. "How was your vacation?"

"Okay, I guess. How about yours?"

"It was fine. I thought you were going to come to the Thanksgiving game at the high school," she said in a disappointed voice.

"Well . . . I was, but something came up," I said. "I had to make the cranberry sauce."

"Sheila, don't lie to me," Ellen said.

I practically dropped the phone. Ellen sounded so angry! "I'm not," I said. But that was a lie, too.

"I know you didn't go because you don't want to see people," Ellen continued. "And I also know I'm getting really sick of it."

I didn't know what to say. "Look, I'm sorry I missed the game, but it's no big deal."

"Yes it is," she said. "I hardly see you at all anymore! You haven't been to any of my games in the last three weeks. You won't go to the mall with me, or to the movies. You don't want to do anything!"

"That's not true," I said. "I've just been busy."

"Give me a break," Ellen replied. "Sheila, it's time you got over what happened on Talent Night. So Ron gonged your act. So he didn't know what he was doing. So what?"

"So what?" I repeated. "So what? So, everyone in the whole school was laughing at me, that's what!"

"No, they weren't! I was there, too, you know. And anyway, that was a long time ago! No one remembers you."

"Oh, thanks, thanks a lot," I said angrily.

"Well, that's what you want, isn't it?"

"Listen, Ellen, you don't understand. You don't know what it's like to be humiliated in public. You always do everything right, you never make mistakes. You don't know how I feel when I see Ron at school! I want to shrivel into a ball and roll away," I told her truthfully.

"That is so typical of you," Ellen said. "You think I don't know what it feels like to embarrass myself in front of a huge crowd? I've fallen down on the soccer field. I've been two feet away from the goal and still missed shots. I was on the team the year it only won two games, remember?" She paused to catch her breath. "I didn't quit the team just because I looked bad in front of all those fans. If I had, I'd never be captain, like I am now!"

"Well, you're perfect and I'm not," I said. My eyes were full of tears that were threatening to roll down my face any second. Ellen and I had never had such a big fight before, not in the whole six years I'd known her. I felt like she hated me! "I guess you don't want to be friends with me anymore, because I'm such a wimp," I said.

"I don't want to be friends if you're not going to be a friend to me," she said. "You've totally deserted me! It's like you don't exist anymore."

A tear trickled down my cheek. "Then I won't be messing things up for you, will I?" I said.

Before she could say anything else, I hung up the phone. I ran into my room, threw myself down on my bed, and started sobbing into the pillow.

No one understood how I felt . . . not even my best friend. My ex-best friend.

CHAPTER

December was incredibly cold, and not just outside, either. I think Ellen talked to me once, and that was because our parents made us get rides home from school together during a snowstorm.

I spent Christmas vacation with my parents, *attempting* to ski in Vermont. I ended up reading a lot of books by the fire, and I drank gallons of hot chocolate. I also wrote an article for the *Gazette* about skiing fashions. I didn't want to, but Susan kept bugging me to submit something. Since I'd never written the one I tried to do over Thanksgiving break, she was really on my case.

Susan said she wanted to publish a special issue that would come out the first week back from winter break. She was going to do most of the paper herself. She wanted to fill it with lists of things kids could do at school during the winter quarter.

Susan actually wanted me to drop my article off at her house before New Year's, so she could get the paper out on the first day back. I didn't know how she was going to do it, unless she spent her New Year's Eve in front of a printing press. But, knowing how organized and dedicated Susan was, it wouldn't be totally unheard of for her.

I was suffering from a major case of cabin fever by the time school started up again. I knew it was my own fault, since I wouldn't do stuff with people. But I couldn't do anything about it. I still felt like I needed to hide. At least winter clothes were good for that. In my big down jacket and wool hat, no one could recognize me. Unfortunately, the halls were a little too warm to walk around like that.

On my way to homeroom, I spotted a pile of *Gazettes* outside the student council office. Susan had finished her special edition after all! I grabbed a copy and opened it to the first page. The first thing I saw made me grimace. It was a half-page ad for the *Grease* auditions. It said, "We need *you!*" in big letters.

No, you don't, I thought.

The auditions were going to be held in two weeks. According to the ad, there was still plenty of time to sign up. And plenty of time not to, I added, laughing to myself as I walked into homeroom. I pitied the poor people who had to get up on that stage. I wouldn't put myself in that position ever again!

I slid into my seat and flipped through the paper, looking for my article. I found it on page three: GOING DOWNHILL FAST, A Look at What's Hot (and Not) on the Slopes, by Sheila Jenkins.

"Wait a minute," I said out loud. By Sheila Jenkins? I stared at the newspaper. "How could this have happened?" The article was supposed to be published under my pen name, Daisy Pritchard!

It looked as though the winter semester was off to just as bad a start as the fall one. I wished I'd never even *heard* of ninth grade.

Right before lunch, I went to Susan's locker to find out what had gone wrong. I couldn't get over the fact that she had betrayed me. I never would have written an article for her stupid special edition if I'd known it was going to be under my name.

"Susan, you promised!" I cried when I saw her standing at her locker. "You said my name wouldn't be anywhere near this article!" I practically threw the *Gazette* in Susan's face.

She turned to face me. "What are you talking about?"

"My article was supposed to be by Daisy Pritchard," I told her. "Not me!"

"Do you know how weird that sounds?" Susan asked with a laugh.

I folded my arms across my chest and stared at her.

"Okay, I'm sorry," Susan said. "I know you wanted to be anonymous. But I had crossed out the phony name and written your real name on top of the article so I'd remember who had written it. Not that I couldn't figure it out, because you have such a unique style. Anyway, that's why the printer put in your name instead," she explained.

"Didn't you proofread the paper when it came out?" I asked.

"Yeah, but unfortunately, it was too late. The schedule was crunched because I wanted to get the paper out today," Susan explained. She shrugged. "I'm sorry, Sheila. Don't worry, though—everyone loves the article. I heard people laughing about it this morning in study hall."

"Yeah, right," I mumbled, giving her a skeptical look.

She shut her locker. "Do you want to go to lunch with me? I thought maybe we could talk about your next article. How about a sequel? Something like 'Skating on Thin Ice,' all about the goofy things people wear when—"

"I don't think so," I said, interrupting her. "I'll see you later." I started to walk away, but I didn't know where I was going. I couldn't very well eat my lunch outdoors in January. But I wasn't going to show my face in the cafeteria, either. Maybe I could get the nurse to send me home on account of incurable embarrassment. Probably not, though. I decided I'd better eat— I'd need my strength later, no doubt.

I was on my way to my locker to get my sandwich when I saw a group of guys standing outside the gym door. I recognized some of them as my "buddies" from the soccer team. They were holding the newspaper and laughing. I took a deep breath and prepared for the worst. If only I could get by without them saying anything!

"Hey, Sheila!" Chip Hopkins called out.

Uh-oh, I said to myself. Just keep your cool.

"Great article!" Chip said as I approached the group.

"Yeah, I like the part about how a bunch of people in neon ski pants look like aliens coming down the mountain to get us," Pete Phelan chimed in.

I took a deep breath—this time to keep from passing out! Were they serious? Were these the same guys who had teased me to death back in November? They actually thought what I wrote was funny—*and* they were telling me?

Chip held up the newspaper and snapped it with his finger. "Finally, something decent in here."

"Yeah, seriously," John Corcoran agreed. "This thing was getting pretty lame."

"Well, um, thanks," I muttered as I walked

by. I didn't want to hang around and push my luck. Right before I turned the corner at the end of the hall, though, I heard Pete reading out loud: "The only reason I can see for wearing goggles like that is in case of a nuclear bomb attack." Then the rest of them cracked up.

Maybe the winter wasn't going to be so bitter after all, I thought as I got my sandwich out of my locker.

I decided to risk eating in the cafeteria. It was pretty crowded, so I didn't think anyone would notice me. I sat over by the windows at a table with a bunch of people I didn't know. I would have liked to sit with Ellen, but we just weren't on good terms. She was with Ruth and Keesha, and they looked like they were having a good time, talking and laughing. I missed Ellen. I still spoke with Ruth and Keesha occasionally, but I got the feeling they had taken Ellen's side.

"This is gross!" a girl at the table suddenly squealed. I glanced over and saw her push her plate away. She had straight blond hair, blue eyes, and a dark tan. I didn't recognize her. Maybe she had just transferred to Midway for the winter term.

"What *is* that?" the boy next to her asked, poking his fork into the food on her plate. I recognized him as one of the drummers from the school band, but I couldn't remember his name. He was kind of cute.

"It's supposed to be macaroni and cheese," the girl said. She made a face. "Yuck!"

"You should have known not to get that," the drummer said. "They make it with floor cleaner."

"What?" the girl cried.

The drummer nodded. "Seriously." He pointed down the table at me. "Ask her!"

I was embarrassed to be caught staring at them, and I could feel my face turning pink. I smiled and looked down at the table.

"She did this great comedy routine all about the rotten food here," the drummer continued. "They had this thing called Talent Night in the fall, only no one had any talent, except her."

I was taking a sip of my diet soda, and I practically choked! Was I so lonely that I was *hearing* things now?

"Yeah, but the judges were incredibly stupid and they gave her the gong instead of first place." He shook his head. "It figures, right?"

"Well, what am I supposed to eat?" the girl asked, frowning at her plate of gluey macaroni.

"Try the brownies," I said, before I could think about what I was doing. They both looked over at me, and I shrugged. "Um, I think they use a mix," I told them. "They can't mess that up."

"Don't be so sure!" the drummer said, winking at me.

"Boy, this makes me miss my old school in

California," the girl said. "At least there the food was edible."

I smiled. For the first time in weeks, I *didn't* want to transfer to another school!

I couldn't believe it. Everyone *didn't* think I was a total idiot. I didn't even know this guy, and he thought my act was okay—no, better than okay. He actually liked it!

Maybe there were other people who felt the same way. Even if there weren't, at least there was one person who didn't think I had acted like a bumbling loser on Talent Night.

Actually, there was more than one person who believed in me. I stood up, stuffed the rest of my lunch in the trash can, and started walking across the cafeteria.

"Hey, Sheila!" someone on my right called. It was Jenny Campbell, a girl in my English class. "Loved your article!"

I stopped in front of her table and smiled. "Thanks!"

"I have a great idea for your next one. How about, 'Why Guys Can't Dress'?" Jenny asked. "I mean, have you ever noticed that they *all* look alike?"

"That's a good idea," I said, nodding. "I'll talk to you later, okay?"

She seemed disappointed when I walked away, but I couldn't help it. I was on a mission!

Unfortunately, the bell on the wall didn't realize that, and it rang just at that moment. Two seconds later, people were running all over the cafeteria to get to their next class, and I missed my chance.

But I knew the first thing I was going to do when school got out that afternoon.

CHAPTER

When Ellen saw me standing in front of her locker, she nearly turned and ran the other way.

I'm not joking. We hadn't really spoken since our big fight, and we'd avoided each other whenever possible. We weren't in any classes together, so that was easy.

She walked up, keeping her distance from me. "Excuse me, I need to get into my locker," she said in an irritated voice, without looking up.

"Tough," I said.

Ellen stepped back. She looked like she was about to punch me.

"Ellen, you can't open your locker until you

do one thing," I went on. "Forgive me. Please?" I asked in a squeaky voice.

She frowned. "Why should I?"

"Because I . . . I didn't know what I was doing," I admitted. "I know I acted like a real jerk after I bombed out at Talent Night. I wanted to come to all of your games, I really did! I just got a little, well—"

"Paranoid?" Ellen interjected.

I nodded. "Among other things."

"A *little* paranoid? How about incredibly, unbelievably, majorly—"

"Okay, okay, I get the point," I said.

"So are you saying you're ready to come out of hiding now?" Ellen asked. She was trying to be mean, but the corners of her mouth kept curling up into a half-smile.

I nodded. "And I'm sorry I got mad at you. You were only trying to help. I just felt . . . I don't know." I shifted my books to my other arm. "I felt like everyone in the whole school was laughing at me. Including you."

"I *was* laughing—at your jokes," Ellen said. "I'm sorry I said I didn't want to be your friend. My life has been *so* boring without you."

"Good," I said.

"Good?" Ellen stared at me. "Thanks a lot!"

"No, no," I said, laughing. "I mean, good, because I've been bored stiff, too!" I held out my hand for Ellen to shake. "Truce?"

She took my hand and squeezed it as hard

as she could, until I said, "Ow!" Then she put her arms around me and we hugged.

"Okay, now that we're both forgiven, let's go to Super Scoop and celebrate." Super Scoop is the best frozen yogurt place in town. It's at the mall, and it's usually packed with kids.

Ellen looked at me and raised one eyebrow. "Sheila, it's about ten degrees outside—do you really want to eat frozen yogurt?"

"We don't have to get it to go, silly. Anyway, we can get a *hot* fudge sundae." I rubbed my stomach. "I'm starving!"

Ellen opened her locker and pulled out her winter jacket. "Yeah, I thought you looked kind of thin."

"I've lost five pounds since we've stopped talking," I told her. "I call it the Ellen Berret Diet." Ellen shut her locker and we started walking down the hall. "The only problem is, you have to give up Ellen Berret to do it. It's not really worth it!"

Ellen hoisted her knapsack over her right shoulder and linked her left arm through mine. "Then I guess you can forget about being a fashion model, huh?"

"Yeah, I guess so," I said with a sigh. Then we both cracked up laughing. It felt great to be back with my best friend!

"That sundae was the best ever," Ellen said, leaning back in her chair at Super Scoop.

"Let's have another," I said.

"Not right away," Ellen said. "Besides, you don't want to gain weight before the auditions, do you?"

I stopped licking my spoon and put it down on the table. "And what auditions would those be?"

"You know what I'm talking about," Ellen said, rolling her eyes. "It's only your most favorite play ever, and I quote."

I wished Ellen didn't remember everything I said. But I guess that's your best friend's job. "Ellen, I'm not auditioning for *Grease*."

"They're still looking for people. Hardly anybody's signed up yet," Ellen said. She leaned forward, across the table. "I heard someone you like is on the list."

"No kidding," I said. "That's great. But I'm not getting up on stage. I told you. I thought I was going to be an actress, but I'm not. I found out I'm not good enough." I took a sip of water. "I had a lot of time to think about things over Christmas break, and I've decided to become a professional wrestler."

Ellen burst out laughing. "Don't you even want to know who else is trying out for the play?"

"It's not called a tryout," I scoffed. "That's for sports teams."

She glared at me. "Will you just listen for a second?"

I sat back in my chair and folded my hands behind my head.

"Number one, you can still be a comedian. You just need to practice more—everyone has had bad opening nights, even famous people. Number two, you don't have the body for wrestling." She stopped and looked around the shop before continuing. "And number three," she said in a whisper, "Ron is trying out, auditioning, whatever." She sat back and smiled.

"So?" I crumpled my napkin into a ball and put it on the table. I didn't want Ellen to know, but the idea of being in the musical with Ron was pretty exciting. Even though he had been a jerk, I still liked him.

"So, you have to," Ellen said. "Look, I know you probably still hate Ron for gonging your act. But that doesn't mean he's not a nice guy."

"It doesn't?" I asked.

"No. I mean, they gonged a bunch of people that night. I think they felt like they had to, because they built it up as this big thing. I can think of a couple of people who were really good and still got gonged. Including you."

I thought about that for a minute. Ellen was right. Some other good acts *had* been gonged by the judges. But why? If my act was really okay, didn't that mean Ron hit the gong because he hated *me*—not the act?

"I did hear someone repeating one of my jokes today," I admitted.

Ellen hit the table with the palm of her hand. "I told you!" she yelled.

Everyone in Super Scoop turned to look at us.

"Nice going, El. Say it a little louder next time," I said out of the corner of my mouth.

She grinned. "So, are you going to sign up again or do I have to do it for you?"

"I'll think about it," I said. "I don't want to rush into anything."

"Like you haven't been thinking about it forever," Ellen said with a sigh.

"Give me a break. I just made up with my best friend. I can't do everything in one day," I told her.

"Well, hurry up," she said. "They're not going to hold up the spring musical for you."

"They're not?" I asked, pretending to be shocked. "Wait until my agent hears about this!"

Ellen giggled. "Same old Sheila."

"You mean, the same old Sheila you know and love," I corrected her. "Speaking of which, I'm still hungry. Want to split another sundae?"

Ellen nodded. "Sure, why not?"

"I guess this means the Ellen Berret Diet is officially over," I said as I stood up to get our second sundae. "I might turn into a blimp, but at least we're friends!"

That night I skipped dinner—I was still full from our pigout at Super Scoop. My parents were thrilled when I told them Ellen and I were hanging out together again. They really like her, I guess, even though when she's over here they're always yelling at us to keep it down or get out of the kitchen or something.

I did my homework quickly. Since it was the first day back, the teachers hadn't given us very much. All in all, I felt pretty happy to be back in school. The first day had been better than the whole fall term.

Even though my schedule had been switched around for the new term, I was still in the same English class as Ron. He had said hello to me that day, and I had said "hi" back. Not exactly a meaningful relationship, but it was better than nothing.

I wasn't sure I could ever live down that image of the talentless girl at Talent Night. Then again, I hadn't really *tried* to live it down, either. I had pretty much given up on impressing Ron—and everyone else at Midway Junior High. Still, some of them had been impressed, by my articles and by my act. It was weird. I didn't know what to do, or think, anymore.

Around nine o'clock, I went downstairs and turned on the TV. There was a videotape I wanted to watch. My parents had bought it for me a few months ago, but I'd hardly watched it at all.

When I heard the opening notes of the first song in *Grease*, I got up and started dancing around the room, singing along with the sound-track.

I heard someone clapping, and I turned around. My mother was standing in the doorway. "That was great!" she said.

I turned down the volume and stood in front of the TV, hoping to shield it from her. "Oh, I was just, um—"

"Practicing for the audition?" she asked with a hopeful look in her eye.

"Well, I'm not so sure about that," I said. "I kind of just wanted to take a look at this tape. You got it for me, and I've never really watched it, and I felt bad, you know."

"Yes, I *do* know." My mother sat down on the arm of the couch. "You're thinking about being in the play again, aren't you?"

Mothers! Why do they have to know everything? "Well . . ."

"Oh, come on, Sheila, do it. I know you can get a part," she said, beaming.

"I might be able to. If I don't forget all my lines this time," I said.

Mom waved her hand in the air. "You don't have to memorize them for the audition—they'll let you read from the script. And you won't be up there by yourself. They'll have you audition with someone else. Piece of cake."

"Piece of cake, huh?" I repeated. "I don't know about that." I turned around and looked at the TV. All the characters were dancing around in cool outfits, smiling and having a great time. If—*if*—I got a part, I'd be able to do that. And if Ron was in the play, too, we'd be doing that together.

"I'll do it," I said softly.

My mother jumped up and hugged me from behind. "All right! One star, coming right up!"

"Mom," I said, frowning. "You make me sound like an egg or something."

As long as I didn't end up with egg on my face again, I didn't have anything to lose by auditioning. Did I? I'd already been embarrassed once in public. The second time couldn't be that bad. Maybe I'd get used to it and even start to like it. It could be a hobby of mine, I thought. I'd be good at being bad.

No, I thought as I watched Sandy walk shyly across the courtyard on the TV screen. I wasn't going to give up yet. *This* time I would be ready. And I'd be good, too.

I hoped.

CHAPTER

The next day, I put my name back on the audition list. Ellen stood beside me for moral support. (Actually, she almost had to write my name for me, I was such a chicken.) Then all I had to do was wait until the big day.

I watched the movie a few more times to get a feel for the different roles. But the play and the movie weren't exactly the same, so I read through the script a few times, too. Ellen says that whenever I do something, I do it to death. I guess she's right.

The auditions were on a Monday afternoon. Ellen came over to my house on Saturday to help me prepare.

"Now, don't laugh if you don't think I'm funny," I warned her when I opened the front door. "I don't want to go through that again."

Ellen flopped onto the big couch in the living room. "Sheila, you didn't write the stupid play. If the lines aren't funny, it's not your fault."

"I guess you're right. Do you want something to drink?" I asked her.

"Sure. How about orange juice?" she said.

I got us both glasses of orange juice and went back to the living room. "The first thing we have to do is some of the exercises from this book," I said, handing her a glass.

"What book?"

I held up the copy of *Conquering Stage Fright* I had taken out from the town library.

"Let me see it," said Ellen. She flipped through the first several pages, and suddenly burst out laughing. "There's a chapter in here called—called—" She was laughing so hard she couldn't get the word out.

"Tell me already," I demanded.

"It's titled, 'Picture the Audience in Their Underwear'!" Ellen finally cried.

"Whose underwear are we talking about?" my father asked, walking in from the kitchen.

"Oh, um, nothing," Ellen said, blushing.

"It's in this book about stage fright," I told my father, giggling as Ellen gave me the book. "The author says to picture the audience in their underwear."

My father nodded. "It works every time for me."

Ellen almost dropped her glass. "Are you serious?"

"Sure. I hate getting up in front of a crowd—"

"So it's genetic!" I cried.

"But I have to do it a lot in my job," my father went on, ignoring my comment. My dad is an engineer and he has to make presentations for clients. "I was always very nervous, until one of my co-workers told me about that trick. It never fails to take away my stage fright. The only problem is, you have to restrain yourself from cracking up. You should see some of my clients!" My father laughed.

"Well, I don't know if I want to use that particular trick," I said, thumbing through the book. "There are lots more in here I could try."

"Yeah, but none that are that funny," Ellen said, still giggling. "Can you imagine Mr. Blackwell?"

"Well, good luck," my father said. "I'm going down to the store to pick up a few things. See you later."

Once he was gone, Ellen and I started doing some of the exercises in the book. She had to time me while I practiced breathing, which seemed kind of ridiculous. Don't we breathe all the time? But I guess when you're nervous you breathe too fast. I didn't want to hyperventilate and sing at the same time.

I read my lines while envisioning a wall where Ellen—my audience—was sitting. I did some of the "positive mental imagery" exercises the book suggested, too.

When we were done with the book, both Ellen and I were so relaxed, we felt like taking a nap!

"Now all you have to do is stay this calm until Monday afternoon," Ellen advised as we went upstairs to my room.

"I wish the auditions were right now," I said. "I just want to get them over with!"

Ellen pointed to the alarm clock beside my bed. "Only forty-eight hours to go."

That scared me: only forty-eight hours until I got back up on that disastrous stage. "It's *not* going to be a disaster," I said out loud.

"What did you say?" Ellen asked, stretching out on my bed.

"Nothing, I was just doing some more posi-tive thinking," I told her.

"Well, keep it up. Remember, B-E—"

"Don't say it," I warned Ellen. I grabbed a pillow and pretended I was going to throw it at her. "Don't you dare say it."

Ellen brushed her hair back from her face. "All I was going to say was be . . . yourself! And you'll do great."

"Nice try," I said, nodding. "But you sound like Mr. Glynn." Mr. Glynn is always giving lec-tures about how we shouldn't worry about fit-ting in. He says we should just be ourselves. We always wondered who else we were supposed to be.

"Just think of how proud Mr. Glynn will be when you star in *Grease*," Ellen said, starting to giggle. "Maybe he'll even be there Monday, and you can picture him—" She gasped for breath. "—in his underwear!"

I burst out laughing. That was definitely one stage fright trick I would have to avoid, unless I wanted to laugh myself right off the stage!

"So, how do you feel?" Ellen asked me. She was waiting for me at my locker after school let out on Monday.

"Okay, I guess. I'm nervous, but I don't think I'll pass out or anything," I told her.

"Of course you won't!" said Ellen. "Just think about all those things the book said. And I'm going to be there, so just pretend we're in your living room."

"Oh, sure," I said. "As if fifty people could fit in my living room." We started walking down the hall toward the auditorium, and my stomach did a few flips.

"The only person you have to impress is Mr. Blackwell," Ellen reminded me. "I happen to know that none of those other people on the audition list is as talented as you."

I smiled at Ellen. "You'd make a great manager. Now all you have to do is start calling me 'babe' and 'honey.' "

"Not a chance," Ellen said as she pulled open the door to the auditorium.

It was funny. I thought being back in the auditorium for the audition would make me feel sick to my stomach, but it didn't. It felt *familiar*, because I'd performed there before—or tried to, anyway. Some of the kids looked familiar, too. A lot of them had participated in Talent Night.

I checked in with Mr. Blackwell, and told him I wanted to audition for the role of Betty Rizzo. She's kind of a tough girl, and she's the head of this group of girls called the Pink Ladies. She's very funny and has a lot of great lines. Rizzo was my favorite character in the movie. Besides, I knew I would never make it as Sandy, the sweet girl Danny falls in love with!

I sat with Ellen while I waited for my turn. There was a pianist who played accompaniment for the singing part of the audition. "What are you going to sing?" Ellen whispered while we listened to a girl belt out, "Freddy, My Love."

"Whatever Mr. Blackwell asks me to, I guess," I said. "Rizzo has two big songs—one's funny and the other's serious. I hope I don't have to do the serious one, because the notes are a lot higher." I was talking about "There Are Worse Things I Could Do," which is a really pretty song. But I didn't exactly have the best vocal pipes in the world. Plus, you always hear about people's voices cracking at auditions. What if mine cracked in front of Ron?

Then I realized something—Ron was nowhere to be seen! I looked all over the auditorium, but I didn't see him anywhere. "Hey, Ellen." I tugged at her sleeve. She was totally engrossed in Brian Sweeney's performance of "Beauty School Dropout." I have to admit, Brian is on the gorgeous side.

"Ellen," I whispered, a little more loudly this time.

"Huh?" She turned to me with a glassy look in her eyes.

"Well, I guess I know who *you* want to cast in the play," I teased her.

"He's a good singer," she said, shrugging.

"Yeah, right. Anyway, guess what? Ron isn't here," I told her.

"He's *not*?" Ellen sat up in her seat and looked around the auditorium.

"Nope. He was in English class this afternoon, so he can't be home sick or anything," I said.

"Maybe he just chickened out," Ellen said.

"I hope not." I glanced around the auditorium again. "Wait a minute, what am I saying? I'm *glad* he's not here." Now I wouldn't have to worry about embarrassing myself. If my audition went well, great. If it didn't, it would be easier to take without Ron sitting there laughing at me. I could just see him sitting next to Mr. Blackwell and making a slashing motion across his throat halfway through my song.

"Sheila Jenkins, you're next!" Mr. Blackwell announced.

I sat up with a start. Once again, it was the moment of truth. Ellen grinned and squeezed my hand. "You'll be great!"

I smiled and walked up to the stage. Brian Sweeney was still there, too. A pile of scripts was lying on the floor, so I took one.

"Please turn to Act One, Scene Three," Mr. Blackwell instructed us. "Sheila will play Rizzo, and Brian will read Kenickie."

I looked out at all the kids watching and took a deep breath. Even though I was supposed to be picturing them in their underwear, I felt like I was the one who was half-dressed!

Still, Brian and I made it through the scene without any major catastrophes. In fact, I thought it went pretty well. I was feeling good about the whole experience until Mr. Blackwell told Brian to leave the stage. Then he asked me to sing "There Are Worse Things I Could Do."

I shot Ellen a panicked look. She grinned confidently and gave me the thumbs-up signal. It helped to know she was there rooting for me. Suddenly I understood why she was so upset with me for not coming to her soccer games. She relied on me, too.

"Ready?" the woman playing the piano asked me.

I nodded and flipped to the page in the script with the lyrics. Even though I knew them by heart, I didn't want to take any chances.

I was halfway through my first line when I saw the door to the auditorium open. And there, walking down the aisle, staring up at me, was none other than Ron Lawson.

My voice didn't crack. It sort of warbled. Then I pretended there was a brick wall between me and Ron and everyone else. Instead of looking out at them, I focused on the piano. I knew you couldn't do that in an actual show, but I hoped it was all right for an audition.

When I finished singing, Mr. Blackwell clapped and said, "Nice job. Thank you very much."

That was the first time anyone had ever *thanked* me for singing. Usually my parents ask me to keep my voice down.

I smiled briefly at Mr. Blackwell, and then walked off the stage. Ron looked at me when I walked past him and sort of gave me a half-smile. At least he wasn't cracking up.

"Well, I didn't get gonged," I said to Ellen when I sat down next to her.

"You were really good," she said excitedly. "I thought you were going to die when Ron walked in."

"I did, too," I admitted. "But what can I say? I'm a seasoned performer."

"Yeah, you're seasoned all right," Ellen said. "Up here!" She pointed to my head.

We stuck around and watched the rest of the auditions. About five other girls auditioned for the part of Rizzo. They all seemed good to me. Ron was one of the last people to get up on stage. He read as Danny, which I personally thought was a mistake. I thought he would make a much better Kenickie. But then, what did I know? This was only my first real audition for a play. Ron's singing was pretty good—he wasn't going to get a record contract with it, but it was okay.

"So," Ellen said when Ron's song ended, "are you still in love with him now that you know he's not perfect?"

I grinned. "What do you mean, he's not perfect?"

"He sounds like he has something stuck in his throat," Ellen said.

"He's probably just nervous," I said. "Anyway, you don't have to be perfect to be in a junior high musical. This isn't Broadway, you know."

"That's what I've been trying to tell you for the last two weeks!" Ellen let out an exasperated sigh. "So what happens next?"

"We wait. The cast list isn't going to be posted until Friday." Friday . . . it seemed like light years away. Did they actually expect us to wait that long? How was I going to make it?

CHAPTER

10

My heart was racing on Friday as I walked down the hall to the drama club office. Actually, *pounding* is more like it. My palms were all sweaty, too—I had dropped my books twice on the way down the hall. I felt like running, but I didn't want to make even more of a fool of myself, especially if my name wasn't on the list.

When I got closer, I saw a bunch of other kids crowded around the office door. Mr. Blackwell had said he would post the list by noon, and it was 11:59.

"Hi, Sheila," Jessica McAllister said, walking up beside me. She had auditioned, too.

"Hi, Jess," I said. "Are you as nervous as I am?"

She nodded and held up two crossed fingers. "I've been holding my fingers like this all morning. They hurt!"

I smiled and we kept walking. When we got up to the door, I could see that the list was already there. People were reading it and then walking away—and most of them did *not* look happy.

"Set designer?" I heard one girl say. "*Set* designer? I wanted to sing, not paint!"

"Uh-oh," Jessica whispered as we moved closer.

I was so hyper I could hardly focus on the list. Wendy Harmon, the terrific singer who had won on Talent Night, had been cast as Sandy. That didn't surprise me very much—she had been so much better than everyone else. The cute guy from the auditions, Brian Sweeney, would be Danny. That meant Ron hadn't gotten the part. And—

"Sheila, you're Rizzo!" Jessica suddenly cried, leaping into the air. "And I'm Frenchy!"

I was so stunned I had to remind myself to breathe. "I'm Rizzo," I said, so that I would believe it. "I'm Rizzo!" I grabbed Jessica's hands and we started dancing around in a circle. "And you're Frenchy!"

"This is going to be great!" she said.

A new bunch of people came up to look at the list, so we stopped dancing and moved out of the way. I didn't want to rub it in if people hadn't gotten the parts they wanted.

Besides, I had to see who else was on the list. I had a lot of scenes with Kenickie, so I wanted to know who I'd be spending my afternoons with for the next—

"Ron Lawson is Kenickie," Jessica whispered to me. "You're so lucky!"

I leaned forward and ran my finger along the list. Kenickie . . . Ron Lawson. I couldn't believe it. "Wow," was all I could say.

"Wow is right. He's adorable," Jessica said. "Remember how he was one of the judges at that awful Talent Night thing?"

"Of course I remember," I said. "He's the one who gonged my act."

"Oh, that night was a total waste anyway," Jessica said with a wave of her hand. "This is going to be completely different. I can't wait for our first rehearsal!"

"Neither can I," I said. I was in a daze as we wandered down the hall to the cafeteria. I had gotten a part in the spring musical! And not just any part—a good one, the one I wanted!

My career on stage wasn't all over, it was just beginning. I still wanted to prove to Ron that I was worth knowing. But maybe getting the part of Rizzo was proof enough!

Jessica and I split up when we got to the cafeteria. I headed right for Ellen, Ruth, and Keesha. Since I had made up with Ellen, we were all friends again.

"Well?" Ellen asked. "What happened?"

I grinned. "You are looking at one of the stars of the spring musical."

Ellen threw down her fork, jumped up, and hugged me. "Congratulations! I knew you could do it!" she cried.

"Yeah, well, I'm glad you did, because I didn't," I told her. "Thanks."

"No problem," she said, sitting back down at the table. "Just don't forget me in that book."

"What book?" asked Keesha.

"Never mind," I told her.

"So what part did you get?" asked Ruth.

"Rizzo, the one I wanted," I replied with a smile.

"Rizzo?" Ruth looked confused. "What kind of name is that? Is that your first name?"

"No, it's Betty," I said, sitting down.

"Then why don't you go by Betty?" Ruth wanted to know. "Not that it's much better than Rizzo. Who made up these names, anyway?"

Ellen and I started laughing. "Ruth, wait for the play, okay?" I said. "Oh, that reminds me. Guess who's playing my sort-of boyfriend?"

Ellen leaned forward in her chair. "No. You're kidding."

I shook my head, grinning. "Ron got the part of Kenickie."

"I can't believe it," Ellen said. "This is better than we'd ever hoped!"

"Well, I was hoping for something like this,"

I admitted. "But I don't know how I'm going to make it through rehearsals with him sitting there watching my every move."

Keesha wiggled her eyebrows. "Sounds okay to me!"

"Yeah, I guess it will be," I said, glancing around the cafeteria for my co-star. I wondered how he would feel when he found out we'd be acting together. He probably wouldn't be as thrilled as I was, but as long as he didn't drop out of the play, I had a chance. A small one, but it was better than none.

I didn't talk to Ron very much during the first month of rehearsals. Mr. Blackwell worked with us separately on lots of things, since most of us had never acted before. (Being a Pilgrim in the second-grade Thanksgiving play didn't really count as serious acting.) It was fun, learning how to play the role and how to project my voice and all that. My singing got a lot better, too, because I had to do voice exercises every day.

Finally, near the end of February, the whole cast started meeting for rehearsals. One afternoon, Ron and I were up on stage together for what seemed like hours, trying to get a scene right.

"You're supposed to *like* Kenickie," Mr. Blackwell told me in an annoyed voice.

I had to bite my lip to keep from laughing. As if I didn't like him! I guess I was trying too hard not to let him see that I did, though, so it seemed as if I hated him. "Okay," I said, nodding.

We started the scene again. It was difficult, because there were all these moves we were supposed to be doing while we talked. We kept bumping into each other.

I looked at Ron and shrugged. "Normally I can walk and talk at the same time," I said, smiling.

He laughed. "I just learned how last year, so I'm still kind of new at it." Then he smiled. His smile is one of the best things about the planet Earth. His blue eyes sparkle and crinkle up at the corners, and then there are his perfect teeth.

"Sheila!" the choreographer, Ms. Graff, called. She's very tall and has long dark hair. Ms. Graff teaches dance at her studio in town, but she had been hired to work with the drama club on *Grease*. "Remember, you *sashay* in front of him, then walk around behind him. Ron, you do the opposite," she instructed us.

"Does that mean I don't get to sashay?" Ron replied.

I started giggling.

"Come on, you two—the afternoon's almost over and we're still on the same scene," Mr. Blackwell said. "Once more! Give it all you've got!"

I guess we did give it all we had, because when we were done, Mr. Blackwell, Ms. Graff, and a bunch of cast members in the auditorium applauded us.

Ron took a big bow. "Thank you so much."

"Very nice—there's a real spark between Rizzo and Kenickie," Mr. Blackwell commented.

I just shuffled off the stage. I didn't want to mess up whatever spark there was between us. I grabbed my jacket and was halfway out the door when I heard someone yell, "Hey, Rizzo! Wait up!"

I stopped and turned around. Ron was walking up the aisle toward me. "How do you like the play so far?" he asked me.

I opened the door and we both walked through. "It's pretty good. I mean, I'm enjoying it."

Ron nodded. "Me, too. I've never done any acting before, really. It's a lot of work!"

"Yeah," I said. I couldn't think of anything else to say. Here it was, my first big moment alone with Ron, and I was speechless. "So, what do you think of the other actors?"

"They're okay. We got the best parts, though," Ron said as we walked out of the school into the cold late afternoon air.

"I think so, too," I said. Not that playing Rizzo would be half as much fun if he weren't Kenickie. We stood on the steps for a minute or two. I would have liked to stick around and talk, if I could think of anything to say, but it was freezing. So I said, "Well, I guess I'll see you tomorrow."

"Yeah, okay," Ron answered. He seemed distracted, and I wondered what he was thinking about. "Which way do you live?" he asked.

I pointed with my mittened hand. He pointed in the other direction and shrugged. "Oh well, see you," he said. I nodded and pulled my hat down over my ears.

I had gone about a block when I heard someone yelling. It was hard to hear who, though, because my hat was so thick. I pulled it off and turned around.

"Rizzo!" Ron was waving to me. "I just had a great idea!"

I waited while he ran up to me. "*Grease* is supposed to take place in 1959, right? But we have no idea what it was like way back then. So I was thinking—"

"We should go to a museum?" I asked him.

"Kind of," he said. "You know that diner on Bridge Street? It's called Fred's Oldies, I think. They play fifties music and they have all this stuff on the walls like old ads and records." Ron shrugged. "I just thought, you know, maybe we should go there and, uh, research our characters."

"You mean, take notes?" I asked.

"No, I mean, eat a burger and drink a shake, dummy," Ron said, grinning.

I was stunned. Ron was actually asking me on a date! Sort of, anyway. "Right now?" I asked.

"Sure, why not?" he said. "We can call our parents when we get there and tell them we're having dinner."

"I can see it now—'Hello, Mom? I won't be home for dinner because I'm stuck in 1959.' "

Ron laughed. "I don't know about you, but I'm freezing. Do you want to go or don't you?"

I pretended to think about it for a few seconds. I didn't want to seem too eager. "Sure thing, Kenickie," I said, using my best Rizzo accent. "What are you waiting for?"

We both started running toward Bridge Street. Ron fell once on the ice but I didn't laugh. That's how nice *I* am.

"Are you telling me what I think you're telling me?" Ellen asked when I called her later that night.

"Ron said he only gonged my act because Marcy told him to," I said. "You know how she and I never really got along, right? She hates my jokes—she has ever since I made one about her in fifth grade."

"That's true. Didn't she call you juvenile once?"

"More than once," I said.

"Even though you and Marcy aren't friends, I didn't think she'd go so far as to ruin your act," said Ellen. "But why did Ron go along with it?"

"He's the vice president, so he has to do stuff like that," I explained. "Anyway, he said he was sorry. He kind of got caught up in the whole evening, too. Everyone was expecting them to gong people, so he did, even when he liked their acts. He said he wanted to tell me before, but he could never get up the nerve. Plus, he said I was never around."

"Oh, really? Gee, I hadn't noticed that," Ellen said in a sarcastic voice. "So what's the deal? Are you guys an item now?"

"No," I told her. "But at least we're friends."

"You still like him though, right?"

"Yeah. He's funny and nice and smart and handsome—you know, the basic four requirements for my boyfriends."

"Sheila, you've never *had* a boyfriend before," Ellen said.

"So, that doesn't mean I don't have standards," I replied, laughing. "I'll see you tomorrow."

"If you want to walk to school with Ron, I'll understand!" Ellen cried just as I was about to hang up the phone.

"Very funny. I'm not going out with him yet," I told her. "But when I am, you'll be the first to know!"

CHAPTER

Our first performance wasn't until the end of April. We were going to do four in all—two each weekend. I thought I would go crazy waiting, but I didn't. At least I wasn't any crazier than I had been back in January. Maybe that wasn't saying much.

Anyway, we rehearsed and rehearsed and rehearsed. I felt as if I knew everyone else's lines, too, by the time opening night rolled around.

Ron and I went out together sometimes, but we weren't a couple in the official sense of the word. It was fun playing a couple on stage, though.

The day of opening night was just like any other. I had to get up and go to school just like everyone else. I couldn't wait until I was a real star—then I'd get pampered! My mom did make banana pancakes for breakfast, though, which was sort of special.

I met Ellen on the corner, as usual, only I was a little early because I was so hyper. I was really happy that it was a beautiful spring day. I didn't want to think about what rain would do to the hairdo I had to wear that night.

"Hi, Rizzo," Ellen said with a grin, when she finally arrived.

"Don't call me that," I said. "It's bad luck."

"I thought Ron called you that all the time," she replied.

"He does, but today's different. We could jinx the show or something," I told her. "I don't want to take any chances."

"It's going to be great," Ellen said, "no matter what you say. The dress rehearsal was fantastic! I never knew there were so many talented people at our school."

"Except for the athletes, like the girls' soccer team, right?" I asked with a grin.

"Well, they are pretty good," she said. "But not as good as you when you sing that Sandra Dee song. I love the way you prance around the stage."

"You make it sound like I'm an animal in the circus," I complained.

Ellen glared at me. "Sheila, you're doing it again."

"What?" I asked innocently.

"Your impression of a paranoid. Cut it out, or suffer the consequences," she warned.

"What are you going to do?"

"I'm going to paint a huge sign and hold it up in the audience tonight. It's going to say, 'Sheila Loves Ron!' " She winked at me, then took off running before I could do anything.

As I chased Ellen down the street, I hoped she wouldn't be sitting in the front row that evening. I could just see her standing up in the middle of the show and telling Ron how much I liked him!

Opening night began in total, utter chaos. All of the girls in the show were using the faculty lounge to get ready. The room was much too small for all of our junk, so it was really crowded.

But the worst thing of all was that people were panicking. I heard things like, "Did anyone see my jacket?" and "I can't find the lipstick!" and "My hair looks terrible!"

I was just trying to keep my cool as I sprayed my hair for the twentieth time.

"Sheila, pass me the hair spray!" Jessica yelled from behind me.

I looked in the mirror at her and tossed the can over my shoulder. "Don't use it all up!" I told her. "We might need some later." I reached up and touched my hair. It felt like cotton candy, and it looked like a wig. I was glad I didn't live in the fifties!

I was nervous, but I was looking forward to finally putting on the show for everyone. We had worked hard, and we were ready. At least I thought we were.

Suddenly I got this knot in my stomach. What if I forgot my lines? I couldn't very well write them on my arm. That hadn't worked the first time, anyway. Mr. Blackwell had said he would be in the wings to prompt us if we needed it. But what if I forgot my lines in one of the musical numbers? I'd never be able to hear him. The musical numbers . . . just thinking about them made my stomach clench even tighter.

So this was what it came down to, I thought, looking in the mirror at my made-up face. I was panicking all over again. I could read all the books in the world on stage fright, but it didn't matter. I was not a born performer. Sure, I could hold my own at rehearsals, but that was different. When it came to show time, I choked.

Ms. Graff stuck her head in the door and yelled, "Everyone backstage! We go on in five minutes!"

I gulped. What was I going to do?

Ms. Graff walked over to me. "Sheila, this is for you." She pulled a yellow rose out from behind her back and handed it to me. There was a card attached to the stem. It said, "Break a leg, and don't be paranoid. You're great! Love, Ellen."

I smiled and felt myself relax. Trust Ellen to keep me calm even when she was nowhere in sight. I leaned forward and put on another coat of pink lipstick.

Jessica touched my shoulder. "Ready?"

I stood up and slipped into my black leather jacket. It had "Pink Ladies" stitched on the back of it, just like Jessica's. I took one last glance at myself in the mirror, decided I looked fine, and said, "Come on, Frenchy. Let's rumble."

Before I knew it, the curtains opened and I was out there for the first number. I didn't have time to stop and think about anything—it was time to start singing!

Everything went off without a hitch. Well, everything I did, anyway. The guy running the spotlights kept messing up, and someone's guitar string broke, and Wendy almost forgot one of her lines, but she remembered just in time.

I could hear the audience laughing, but I didn't notice them that much. When I was offstage, in the wings, I thought I would try to find out who was out there. But I ended up watching the other actors instead! I really admired everyone in the production. They were all so good.

While I was standing there watching a scene and waiting for my turn to go back on, I felt someone tug at my jacket sleeve. "Hey, Riz."

I turned and smiled at Ron. "Hey, Kenickie," I said. "How's it going?"

"You were great doing 'Look at Me, I'm Sandra Dee,' " Ron said. "I wish I could sing so well."

"You can," I told him.

Ron shook his head. "No, I don't have a great voice. I think after this I'll only be in non-musicals."

"Don't say that! Then we won't be in any more shows together," I said. Whoops, I thought to myself. I had answered that a little too quickly.

"That's definitely the down side," he agreed, frowning. "But maybe we can see each other, you know, other places."

I chewed my lower lip. Was he saying what I thought he was saying? It was just my luck to like a guy who couldn't come right out and say what he meant. I decided I'd have to take charge of the situation if I ever wanted to be more than friends. "Ron, does that mean—"

"Sheila, Ron, you're on in one minute!" Mr. Blackwell told us.

"What were you going to say?" Ron asked me.

"I'll tell you later," I said. I took the lipstick out of my pocket and put on a fresh coat. "How do I look?" I asked Ron, patting my hair.

"Great, as usual," he said.

The scene ended and the lights dimmed so we could run out on stage. Ron took my hand.

I thought I was going to pass out—not from stage fright, but from shock! Not only had Ron said he liked my looks, but he was holding my hand, too.

There were *definitely* worse things I could do than end up with Ron Lawson for a boyfriend!

"You were wonderful!" my mother cried when she came backstage for our cast party. She ran up and threw her arms around me.

My father hugged me, too, then handed me a big bouquet of red roses. "For the rising star," he said. "We're really proud of you, kid."

"That's my dad's Bogart imitation," I told Ellen, "in case you couldn't tell."

She laughed. "I can't believe how cool you looked up there. You didn't seem nervous at all."

"She's a pro," said my father, putting his arm around my shoulders.

"I was dying right before the show, actually. I started having these Talent Night flashbacks. Then I got your note. Thanks," I said, smiling at Ellen. "You saved my life."

"Well, I didn't want to have you hibernating for another two months," Ellen said with a laugh. "Besides, I knew *you* knew you could do it. You just forget sometimes." She leaned closer and whispered, "By the way, you and Ron looked great together."

I nodded. "I know."

Ellen stepped back and stuck her chin up in the air. "Oh, so now you're getting conceited!"

"No, I'm not!" I punched her in the arm.

My parents left us to mingle with some of their friends whose kids were in the play. While Ellen went off to get some punch, Ron came up to me. "Not bad for the first backstage party," he said.

"Yeah, it's okay. Where are all the reporters?" I joked.

"Didn't they tell you? You have to act in the play and review it, too," he said.

"No problem. I give it four stars," I said. "I especially liked the actors who portrayed Rizzo and Kenickie. They were excellent." I paused. "Especially Kenickie."

"No, I think Rizzo was better," Ron argued, shaking his head. "Kenickie only looked good because he was next to her."

I looked at him. "Do you really mean that?"

He nodded. "It's a fact."

"Well, in that case we'd better stick together," I said with a shrug. "I don't want to make you look bad."

A smile spread across Ron's face. "Okay, it's a deal."

Ellen came back with three glasses of punch—she had seen Ron talking to me—and we drank a toast to our debut. I couldn't wait to tell her about the "deal" Ron and I had made to see each other.

All things considered, ninth grade had turned

out to be a pretty good year. No, it was better than that, I thought as I watched Ellen and Ron laughing together.

I'd have to give it five stars. Maybe six.